"So you think you're safe? Or do we need to run now?"

She gaped at him. "We?" She shook her head. "Even if I'm compromised, you didn't vouch for me. Whatever happens to me, I won't betray your cover. This is about me."

"No, it's not. We're a team now, you and me."

The idea flooded her with warmth, made her feel more secure and more afraid at the same time.

If this was just about her, she wouldn't hesitate. It was worth the risk.

But it was no longer just about her. "I don't think he's going to say anything, but I can't be positive."

Marcos nodded, stepping a little closer. "Nothing in life is a guarantee, especially in undercover work."

Her pulse picked up again at his nearness, her body wanting to lean into him. "What do you think we should do?"

"If you don't think you're compromised, we stay."

If she stayed here much longer, she was definitely going to be compromised, but in a completely different way.

Acknowledgments

Thank you to Paula Eykelhof, Kayla King, Denise Zaza and everyone involved with *Secret Agent Surrender* behind the scenes. Thanks to my family and friends for their endless support, with a special thanks to: Kevan Lyon, Chris Heiter, Robbie Terman, Andrew Gulli, Kathryn Merhar, Caroline Heiter, Kristen Kobet, Ann Forsaith, Charles Shipps, Sasha Orr, Nora Smith and Mark Nalbach.

SECRET AGENT SURRENDER

Elizabeth Heiter

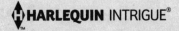

For Andrew—I couldn't have imagined a better real-life hero.
I love you!

Recycling programs
for this product may
not exist in your area.

ISBN-13: 978-0-373-75695-7

Secret Agent Surrender

Copyright © 2017 by Elizabeth Heiter

Printed in U.S.A.

Elizabeth Heiter likes her suspense to feature strong heroines, chilling villains, psychological twists and a little romance. Her research has taken her into the minds of serial killers, through murder investigations and onto the FBI Academy's shooting range. Elizabeth graduated from the University of Michigan with a degree in English literature. She's a member of International Thriller Writers and Romance Writers of America. Visit Elizabeth at www.elizabethheiter.com.

Books by Elizabeth Heiter

Harlequin Intrigue

The Lawmen: Bullets and Brawn

Bodyguard with a Badge
Police Protector
Secret Agent Surrender

The Lawmen

Disarming Detective
Seduced by the Sniper
SWAT Secret Admirer

Visit the Author Profile page at Harlequin.com for more titles.

CAST OF CHARACTERS

Marcos Costa—Deep undercover on a DEA operation, Marcos crosses paths with his first crush, Brenna Hartwell, and he's smitten all over again. The problem is, she might have set the fire that separated him and his foster brothers as kids—and when this operation is over, he'll have to arrest her.

Brenna Hartwell—The rookie police officer is in way over her head when she runs into Marcos again at a drug lord's hideaway. She's onto something big that could change everything they know about the fire, and getting to the truth means getting close to Marcos. Only, if she gets too close, their covers could be blown—and then they're both dead.

Cole Walker—Marcos's eldest foster brother is a police detective, but the role he's always taken most seriously is "big brother" and he's there whenever Marcos needs him.

Andre Diaz—Marcos's elder foster brother is a sniper for the FBI. Like Cole, he'll do whatever it takes to keep Marcos safe when he tries to unravel a decades-old secret.

Carlton Wayne White—The drug lord has been gaining power for nearly twenty years, and Brenna suspects he's doing it on the backs of foster kids.

Jesse White—Carlton's nephew was orphaned and left in Carlton's care. He's Marcos's in at the drug lord's hideaway, but could a secret from his own past ruin the undercover operation?

Dear Reader,

Thanks for joining me for the final book in The Lawmen: Bullets and Brawn miniseries. As children, Cole Walker, Andre Diaz and Marcos Costa formed their own family. Now these brothers try to unravel the secret that separated them so many years ago. Andre's and Cole's stories hit shelves over the last two months, and the miniseries finishes with the youngest brother, Marcos.

If you missed the first Lawmen miniseries, you can find out more about all of the lawmen at my website, www.elizabethheiter.com. You can also learn more about my Profiler series, and my FBI profiler, Evelyn Baine, whose latest case involves the mysterious disappearance of a teenager who left behind a note foretelling her own death.

Thanks for reading! I hope you enjoy Marcos and Brenna's story!

Elizabeth Heiter

Chapter One

"This is a bad idea," Marcos Costa muttered as he drove the flashy convertible the DEA had provided him into the middle of Nowhere, Maryland. Or rather, *up* into the middle of nowhere. He could actually feel the altitude change as he revved the convertible up this unpaved road into the Appalachian Mountains.

"It was your idea," his partner's voice returned over the open cell-phone line.

"Doesn't make it a good one," Marcos joked. The truth was, it was a brilliant idea. So long as he lived through it.

The DEA had been trying to get an in with Carlton Wayne White for years, but the man was paranoid and slippery. Until now, they hadn't even had an address for him.

That was, assuming the address Marcos was heading to now actually did turn out to be Carlton's mansion and not an old coal mine where a drug lord could bury the body of an undercover agent whose cover was blown. Namely, his.

"According to the GPS, I'm close," Marcos told his partner. "I'm going to hide the phone now. I'm only going to contact you on this again if I run into trouble."

"Be careful."

"Will do." Marcos cut the call, hoping he sounded confident. Usually, he loved the thrill of an undercover meet. But this wasn't their usual buy-bust situation, where he'd show up, flash a roll of money, then plan the meet to get the drugs and instead of doing a trade, pull his badge and his weapon. Today, he'd been invited into the home of a major heroin dealer. And if everything went like it was supposed to, he'd spend the entire weekend there, being wined and dined by Carlton.

Because right now, he wasn't Marcos Costa, a rising star in the DEA's ranks. He was Marco Costrales, major player in the drug world. Or, at least, aspiring major player in the drug world, with the kind of money that could buy a front-row seat in the game.

Pulling over, Marcos slid the car into Park and popped open a hidden compartment underneath the passenger seat. Ironically, the car had originally belonged to a dealer down in Florida, and the compartment had been used to hide drugs. Today, Marcos turned off his cell phone to save the battery and slipped it in there, hoping he wouldn't need it again until he was safely out of the Appalachians.

This was way outside normal DEA protocol, but Carlton Wayne White was a big catch, and Marcos's partner was a fifteen-year veteran with a reputation as a maverick who had some major pull. Somehow, he'd convinced their superiors to let them run the kind of op the agency hadn't approved in decades. And the truth was, this was the sort of case Marcos had dreamed about when he'd joined the DEA.

"Let's do this," Marcos muttered, then started the car again. The dense foliage cleared for a minute, giving him an unobstructed view over the edge of the mountain. His breath caught at its beauty. He could see for miles, over peaks and valleys, the setting sun casting a pink-and-orange glow over everything. Carlton Wayne White didn't deserve this kind of view.

Then it was gone again, and Marcos was surrounded by trees. The GPS told him to turn and he almost missed it, spotting a narrow dirt trail at the last second. He swung the wheel right, giving the convertible a little gas as the trail got steeper. It seemed to go on forever, until all of a sudden it leveled out, and there in front of him was an enormous modern home surrounded by an ugly, electrified fence.

Most of the people who lived up here were in that transitional spot between extreme poverty and being able to eke out a living to support themselves. They had a reputation for abhorring outsiders, but rumor had it that Carlton had spread a little cash around to earn loyalty. And from the way the DEA had been stonewalled at every attempt to get information on him, it seemed to have worked.

Marcos pulled up to the gate, rolled down his window and pressed the button on the intercom stationed there. He'd passed a major test to even be given this address, which told him that his instincts about the source he'd been cultivating for months had been worth every minute. "Hey, it's Marco. Here to see Carlton. He's expecting me."

He played it like the wealthy, aspiring drug dealer they expected him to be, entitled and a little arrogant. His cover story was that he came from major family money—old organized crime money—and he was looking to branch out on his own. It was the sort of connection they all hoped Carlton would jump on.

There was no response over the intercom, but almost instantly the gates slid open, and Marcos drove inside. He watched them close behind him and tried to shake off the foreboding that washed over him. The sudden feeling that he was never going to drive out again.

Given the size of his operation, the DEA knew far too little about how Carlton worked, but they did know one thing. The man was a killer. He'd been brought up on charges for it more than once, but each time, the witnesses mysteriously disappeared before he could go to trial.

"You've got this," Marcos told himself as he pulled to a stop and climbed out of the convertible.

He was met by his unwitting source, Jesse White. The man was Carlton's nephew. Jesse's parents had died when he was seventeen and Carlton had taken him in, provided him with a home and pulled him right into the family business. Unlike Carlton, Jesse had a conscience. But he was desperate to prove himself to the uncle who'd given him a home when no one else would. Marcos had spotted it when he'd been poring over documents on all the known players. He'd purposely run into Jesse at a pool bar and slowly built that friendship until he could make his approach.

"Hey, man," Jesse greeted him now. The twenty-four-year-old shifted his weight back and forth, his hands twitching. He was tall and thin, and usually composed. Today, he looked ready to jump at the slightest noise.

Please don't get cold feet, Marcos willed him. Jesse didn't know Marcos's true identity, but that didn't matter. If things went bad and his uncle found out Jesse had brought an undercover agent to his house, being a blood relative wouldn't save the kid.

Marcos tried not to feel guilty about the fact that when this was all over, if things went *his* way, Jesse would be going to jail, too. Because Marcos also saw something in Jesse that reminded him of himself. He knew what it was like to have no one in the world to rely on, and he knew exactly how powerful the loyalty could be when someone filled that void. In Jesse's case, the person who'd filled it happened to be a deadly criminal.

Marcos had gotten lucky. After spending his entire life in foster care, being shipped from one home to the next and never feeling like he belonged, he'd finally hit the jackpot. In one of those foster homes, he'd met two boys who'd become his chosen brothers. He wasn't sure where he would have wound up without them, but he knew his path could have ended up like Jesse's.

Shaking off the memory, Marcos replied,

"How's it going?" He gave Jesse their standard greeting—clasped hands, chest bump.

"Good, good," Jesse said, his gaze darting everywhere. "Come on in and meet my uncle."

For a second, Marcos's instinct was to turn and run, but he ignored it and followed Jesse into the mansion. They walked through a long entryway filled with marble and crystal, where they were greeted by a pair of muscle-bound men wearing all-black cargo pants and T-shirts, with illegally modified AK-47s slung over their backs.

One of them frisked Marcos, holding up the pistol he'd tucked in his waistband with a raised eyebrow.

"Hey, man, I don't go anywhere without it," Marcos said. A real aspiring dealer with mob connections wouldn't come to this meet without a weapon.

The man nodded, like he'd expected it, and shoved the weapon into his own waistband. "You'll get it back when you leave."

Marcos scowled, acting like he was going to argue, then shrugged as if he'd decided to let it go. The reality was that so far, things were going as expected. Still, he felt tense and uneasy.

Then Jesse led him down a maze of hallways probably meant to confuse anyone who didn't know the place well. Finally, the hallway opened into a wide room with a soaring ceiling, filled with modern furniture, artwork and antiques, some of which Marcos could tell with a brief glance had been illegally obtained.

From the opposite hallway, a man Marcos recognized from his case files appeared. Carlton Wayne White was massive, at nearly six-and-a-half-feet tall, with the build of a wrestler. His style was flamboyant, and today he wore an all-white suit, his white-blond hair touching his shoulders. But Marcos knew not to let Carlton's quirks distract him from the fact that the drug dealer was savvy and had a bad temper.

"Marco Costrales," Carlton greeted him, appraising him for a drawn-out moment before he crossed the distance between them and shook Marcos's hand.

Marcos wasn't small—he was five-nine—and made regular use of his gym membership, because he needed to be able to throw armed criminals to the ground and hold them down while he cuffed them. But this guy's gigantic paw made Marcos feel like a child.

"Welcome," Carlton said, his voice a low baritone. "My nephew tells me you're in the market for a business arrangement."

"That's right. I'm looking—"

"No business yet," Carlton cut him off. "This

weekend, we get to know one another. Make sure we're on the same page. Things go well, and I'll set you up. Things go poorly?" He shrugged, dropping into a chair and draping his beefy arms over the edges. "You'll never do business again."

He gave a toothy smile, then gestured for Marcos to sit.

That same foreboding rushed over Marcos, stronger this time, like a tidal wave he could never fight. He could only pray the current wouldn't pull him under. He tried to keep his face impassive as he settled onto the couch.

Then Carlton snapped his fingers, and three things happened simultaneously. Jesse sat gingerly on the other side of the couch, a tuxedo-clad man appeared with a tray bearing flutes of champagne and a woman strode into the room from the same direction Marcos had come.

Marcos turned to look at the woman, and he stopped breathing. He actually had to remind himself to start again as he stared at her.

She was petite, probably five-four, with a stylish shoulder-length bob and a killer red dress. She had golden brown skin and dark brown eyes that seemed to stare right inside a man, to his deepest secrets. And this particular woman knew his deepest secret. Because even though it wasn't possible—it couldn't be—he knew her.

"Meet Brenna Hartwell," Carlton said, his voice bemused. "I can see you're already smitten, Marco, but don't get too attached. Brenna is off-limits."

It *was* her. Marcos flashed back eighteen years. He'd been twelve when Brenna Hartwell had come to the foster home where he'd lived for five years. The moment he'd seen her, he'd had a similar reaction: a sudden certainty that his life would never be the same. His very first crush. And it had been intense.

Too bad a few months later she'd set their house on fire, destroying it and separating him from the only brothers he'd ever known.

After all these years, he couldn't believe he'd recognized her so instantly. He prayed that she wouldn't recognize him, but as her eyes widened, he knew she had.

"Marcos?" she breathed.

And his worst nightmare came true. His cover was blown.

Chapter Two

Marcos Costa.

Brenna couldn't stop herself from staring. Fact was, she might have been drooling a little.

What were the chances? She hadn't seen him since she was eleven years old, a few short months after her whole world had been destroyed and she'd found herself dropped into a foster home. She'd still been reeling from her mother's death, still been physically recovering herself from the car crash that had taken her only family away from her. She'd walked into that foster home, terrified and broken and alone. And the first person she'd seen had been Marcos.

Back then, he'd been twelve, kind of scrawny, with dimples that dominated his face. Even through her devastation, she'd been drawn to him. To this day, she couldn't say quite what it was, except that she'd felt like her soul had recognized him. It sounded corny, even in her own head, but it was the best she'd ever been able to understand it.

Now, there was nothing scrawny about him. Next to Carlton, sure, anyone looked smaller, but this grown-up version of Marcos was probably average height. It was hard to tell with him sitting, but one thing she could see quite well was that he'd filled out. Arms that had once resembled twigs were now sculpted muscle, easily visible through his polo shirt.

And the dimples? They were still there, like the cherry on top of an ice-cream sundae. The man looked like a movie star, with his full, dark head of hair and blue-gray eyes that popped against his pale skin. And just like when she'd been eleven, she couldn't stop staring into those eyes, feeling like she could happily keep doing it for hours.

"You two know each other?"

Brenna snapped out of her daze, realizing Carlton was glancing between them suspiciously as Marcos told her, "Marc-OH. My name is Marco."

"Marco," she repeated dumbly, still wondering what in the world he was doing here. Of all the ways she'd imagined running into him again, in the middle of the mountains at a drug lord's lair certainly wasn't one of them.

And if she didn't get her act together fast, she was going to get both of them killed.

Brenna tried to clear the dazed expression from her face. "Sort of," she answered Carlton, wishing her voice had come out as breezy as she'd intended, instead of breathless.

She glanced back at Marcos, praying whatever he was doing here, he'd leave before he could ruin things for her. This was a once-in-a-lifetime opportunity, and she wasn't going to let it slip away, not even for the first boy who'd made her heart race and her palms sweat.

She strode through the enormous room, her too-high heels clicking against the marble floor, and then settled onto the chair next to Carlton. "I picked him up at a bar. When was it? A couple of years ago?" She shook her head, letting out a laugh, hoping Marcos would go along with her story.

She could have told them she'd known Marcos from the foster home. Carlton knew her history—at least the version of it she'd chosen to let him hear—and he definitely knew about her time at that foster home. But Marcos was using a fake name, and she didn't know what his game was, but she didn't want to contradict whatever story he'd given Carlton. Because no matter how much her heart hurt at the idea of the adult Marcos being a criminal, she held out hope that he was here for some other reason. And she definitely didn't want to cause his death.

"Sorry for telling you my name was Crystal," she said to Marcos.

Carlton guffawed and relaxed again. "Lucky man," he told Marcos.

Marcos's gaze lingered on her a moment longer before he looked back at Carlton. "Yeah, until she slipped out at dawn. But you never forget a face like that." His eyes darted back to her for a split second, and then he accepted the glass of champagne the butler held out.

Brenna relaxed a tiny bit. She shook her head at the butler when he stopped in front of her and simply watched as Carlton, Jesse and Marcos toasted to a potential friendship.

Disappointment slumped her shoulders. She knew what a "potential friendship" toast meant. Marcos Costa was a drug dealer.

She should have recognized it instantly. There weren't very many reasons someone would come out to Carlton Wayne White's secret mansion. To even earn an invite, Marcos had to have some serious connections.

But Brenna couldn't help herself. She looked at him now and she still saw the boy who had opened the door for her, taken her pathetic suitcase in one hand, and her hand in the other.

That foster home hadn't been anything close to a real second home to her, but she'd realized after being sent away a few months later that she'd gotten very, very lucky at that first introduction to life in the system. She'd gotten very, very lucky meeting Marcos.

She'd spent most of the rest of her life dreaming of him whenever things got tough, creating a fiction where she'd see him again and he'd sweep her off her feet. She knew it was ridiculous, but that didn't matter. The dream of Marcos Costa had gotten her through the worst times in her life.

It made her sad to see that he'd grown up into someone who'd have a "potential friendship" with the likes of Carlton Wayne White. Of course, what must he think of her? She wondered suddenly if he'd ever suspected she'd set the fire eighteen years ago that had separated them.

Why would he? Brenna shook it off and tried to focus. She couldn't let Marcos Costa—whatever his agenda—distract her.

She'd worked hard to get this invite to Carlton's house. She'd spent weeks planning ways to catch his attention, then even more weeks testing those theories, until finally he'd taken the bait. But Carlton hadn't gotten to where he was by being careless, or being easily distracted by a woman who wanted to trade assets. She knew he didn't trust her yet. And there was only so far she was willing to go to earn that trust.

But she needed to get close to him, so she could dig up his secrets as thoroughly as she knew he'd tried to look into hers. Because the events of that day eighteen years ago, when the study had gone up in flames around her, still haunted her. And she suspected that Carlton Wayne White, whether he knew it or not, was connected to that day. And that meant he was connected to her. He just didn't know it yet.

If everything went as planned, he wouldn't know it until it was far too late.

THREE HOURS LATER, after a ridiculously heavy five-course meal filled with meaningless small talk, Brenna walked gingerly toward the room Carlton had put her in. Her feet were killing her. The shoes he'd bought her boasted a label she'd never be able to afford, but as good as they looked, they were far from comfortable. Give her tennis shoes over these heels any day of the week. But she'd never tell him that.

Carlton had bought her the dress, too, as well as a necklace that probably cost more than her car. So far, he seemed to be respecting her boundaries: she'd made it clear that she wasn't interested in being anyone's mistress. But she'd also dropped hints that she liked the sort of life her job with the state could never give her.

Slowly, over the course of a series of dinner meet-ups where she'd pretended to be naive enough to think he was interested in simple friendship, he'd dropped his own hints about what he could offer her. About what she might offer him in return.

And now here she was, at his mansion, far from help if he discovered her real intentions, being "interviewed" as clearly as Carlton was doing to Marcos.

Marcos. It had been hard to keep her eyes off him during dinner, a fact she was sure Carlton hadn't missed. Even if Marcos hadn't been her first childhood crush, he was exactly her type. Or at least, he would have been if he weren't a drug dealer.

Besides his good looks, the man was charming and funny and interesting. Maybe a little more cocky and entitled than she'd have expected, but then again, never in a million years would she have pegged that he'd grow up and fall into crime.

He'd seemed so well-adjusted those few months she'd known him, doing well in his classes, having a clear bond with two older boys in the house, a brotherhood that went beyond blood. What had happened to him after that fire?

She knew he and his brothers had been torn apart. All six foster kids had been sent to different places. But that was all she knew; she'd thought about looking him up more than once over the years, but she'd never done it. Now, she almost wished she didn't know the path he'd chosen.

Was it her fault? If she hadn't walked into the study when she had, if that fire hadn't started, would he have traveled a different path?

"Brenna."

The soft voice behind her startled her, and Brenna stepped sideways on her stiletto. She would have fallen except a strong hand grabbed her waist. For a moment, her back was pressed against a ripped, masculine frame she didn't have to see to instinctively recognize.

She regained her balance, her pulse unsteady as she spun and found Marcos standing inches away from her. This close, she should have seen some imperfection, but the only thing marring those too-handsome features was the furrow between his eyebrows. It sure looked like disappointment.

Her spine stiffened, and she took a small step backward. "Marcos, uh, Marco." She glanced around, seeing no one, but that didn't mean much. Carlton was notoriously paranoid. For all she knew, he had cameras inside his house as well as around the perimeter.

Marcos must have had the same thought, because his words were careful as he told her, "I never expected to see you again after that night. And now you're with Carlton, huh?"

All through dinner, she could see Marcos trying to figure out her relationship with Carlton. The drug kingpin had seen it, too, because he'd made offhand comments that implied she was his, without being so obvious she'd be forced to correct him. But apparently, Marcos had bought it.

She flushed at the idea that he thought she was sleeping with a drug lord for jewelry and cars. But she also heated at the idea of keeping up the ruse that she'd spent a night in Marcos's bed.

What would that be like? Her thoughts wandered, to the two of them, sweaty, limbs tangled on the huge bed in her room. She shook it off, but it must not have been fast enough, because when she focused on Marcos again, the look he was giving her told her he'd imagined it, too.

"Uh, no. Carlton and I aren't dating, if that's what you're asking."

"I'm not sure that's what I'd call it," Marcos replied softly.

She scowled at him. "We have a business arrangement, and it's not what you think, so stop looking at me like that. The fact is, my arrangement with him is probably not all that different from yours."

Except it was. The ruse she was running with Carlton was about access, not drugs. If she really planned to go through with what she'd promised him, though, it was probably worse than dealing drugs.

His eyes narrowed on her, studying her with a too-keen gaze, and she tried not to squirm. He had the look of a lot of criminals who made it long enough to build an empire—or so she'd come to believe in her limited experience. Oddly, it was a similar probing look that cops used.

"So, Brenna, what do you do when you're not hanging out in Carlton's mansion, wearing spectacular dresses?" Marcos asked, shifting his weight like he was getting comfortable for a long chat.

The urge to fidget grew stronger. Lying didn't come naturally to her, as much as she'd tried to convince her superiors that she could do it—that she could do *this*, come into a drug lord's home and lie to him over an entire weekend, get him to give her insight and access. She'd actually felt pretty confident—well, a careful balance of confidence and determination—until Marcos had shown up. Now, she just felt off balance.

"I work for the foster care system." She kept up the story she'd given Carlton. "I grew up in the system," she added, even though he knew that. But it was more a reminder to herself: always act as though Carlton or one of his thugs was watching. "And I wanted to be on the other side of it, make some changes."

Marcos tipped his head, his eyes narrowing, like he suspected she was lying, but he wasn't sure about what.

She longed to tell him the whole truth, but that was beyond foolish, and one more sign that her boss was right. She wasn't ready for undercover work, wasn't ready for an assignment like this.

If she told Marcos the truth, she'd be dead by morning.

Still, she couldn't help wondering what he'd say. The words lodged in her throat, and she held them there.

I'm a cop.

Chapter Three

Brenna Hartwell was lying to him.

Marcos didn't know exactly what she was lying about, but he'd been in law enforcement long enough to see when someone was doing it. And not just to him, but to Carlton, too. He prayed the drug boss didn't realize it.

"What do you do for the foster care system?" he asked, wondering if even that much was true.

She fidgeted, drawing his attention to the red dress that fit her like a bandage, highlighting every curve. She was in great shape. Probably a runner. Or maybe a boxer, given the surprising muscle tone he'd felt when he'd grabbed her to keep her from stumbling in her shoes.

"Right now, placement," she said, but something about the way she said it felt rehearsed. "But I'm trying to get them to start a program to help kids transition out of the system."

It was a notoriously tricky time. Kids who spent their lives in foster care hit eighteen and that was it. They were on their own, and they had to learn to sink or swim without any help pretty fast.

Some—like Marcos's oldest brother Cole—did whatever it took. Cole had taken on two jobs, built up his bank account until he could afford an apartment big enough for three. Then when Marcos and his other older brother Andre had been kicked out of the system, they'd actually had a home waiting for them.

But Marcos was lucky. And he knew it. Most foster kids didn't have that. Most kids found themselves suddenly searching for shelter and a job. Tons ended up instantly homeless, and plenty took whatever work they could get, including something criminal.

Had that been what had really happened to Brenna? When she'd shown up on their foster home doorstep that day eighteen years ago, her chin up, blinking back tears, his heart had broken for her. A few months later, she'd been gone. He'd always wondered where she'd ended up, but he'd been too afraid to search for her.

Some kids got lucky, ended up in foster homes with fantastic parents who ultimately adopted them. Others, like him, bounced around from one foster home to the next, from birth until eighteen. He supposed he'd never searched for her because he'd always wanted to believe she'd been one of the lucky ones.

"What about you?" Brenna asked, and he was surprised to hear the wary disappointment in her tone.

She was in Carlton's house because she could offer him something. If it wasn't sex, like Carlton had been implying over dinner, then it was some kind of criminal connection. So, who was she to judge *his* motives?

Still, he felt a little embarrassed as he gave his cover story, the way a real dealer would. "Carlton and I share similar business interests. We're talking about a transaction, but I need to pass his test first." He gave her a lopsided grin. "How do you think I'm doing so far?"

She shrugged. "I wouldn't know. I think you and I are in similar positions."

Interesting. So her association with Carlton was relatively new. He wondered if he could get her out of here when he left, convince her to move her life onto a different track. Maybe all she needed was a little help.

It was a thought Marcos knew could get him killed. Doing anything to disrupt Carlton's life before he committed to the deal and Marcos could slap cuffs on him threatened the whole operation. But the idea hung on, refusing to let go.

For years, he'd had an image of Brenna Hartwell in his mind: a perfect, grown-up version of the little girl who'd made his heart beat faster. And even though she probably couldn't have lived up to that fantasy even if she weren't a criminal, he was still drawn to her in a way he couldn't really explain.

"I should go to bed," Brenna said, interrupting his thoughts. She stared a minute longer, like she wanted to say something, but finally turned and headed off to her room.

All the while, he longed to call after her, longed to ask her why she'd set that fire eighteen years ago. Instead, he watched her go until the door near the end of the hallway clicked quietly shut behind her.

Then Marcos headed to his own room, down a different hallway. He'd just turned the corner when Carlton pushed away from the wall, out of the shadows, nearly making Marcos jump.

The drug kingpin's eyes were narrowed, his lips tightened into a thin line. "Maybe I didn't make myself clear at dinner," Carlton said, his voice low and menacing, almost a snarl. "So, let me be plain. Stay away from Brenna. Or our business here is finished before we get started."

"She's a rookie!"

"Sir, she's determined. She dug all this up on Carlton Wayne White herself. She's found an angle we never even considered and I think it's going to work. She—"

"She's got no undercover experience."

"No, but we can give her a crash course. She's smart. We've never gotten this close to him before."

"I don't like it. And the DEA wants this guy for themselves. They won't be happy if we jump into their territory."

"So don't tell them. It doesn't have anything to do with drugs anyway. Not really."

"Hartwell could get herself killed."

Brenna had overheard the conversation last month, between the chief at her small police station and her immediate boss, the guy who'd convinced her to join the police force in the first place. Victor Raine was the closest thing she had to a friend on the force. She'd met him years ago, when she'd first gotten out of foster care and gone to a presentation on job opportunities. He'd been there, talking about police work, and she'd gone up and asked him a bunch of questions.

Ultimately, when she'd gotten a surprise college scholarship offer that covered not just her tuition, but also part of her lodging, she'd chosen that instead. But years later, after she'd graduated and bounced from job to job without feeling fulfilled, she'd looked Victor up. She'd visited him at the station, and somehow found herself applying to the police academy.

Before she knew it, she had graduated and was a real, sworn-in police officer. It was scarier—and better—than she'd ever expected. But typical rookie patrol assignments had lost their luster quickly, and she'd started digging for more.

Her plan to infiltrate Carlton's network had come to her by accident. She'd been on foot patrol with her partner, a newbie right out of the academy, barely out of his teens. Next to him, her six months of experience had seemed like a lifetime. They'd gotten a call about a disturbance, and when they'd arrived, they'd found a kid stabbed and left for dead on the street.

She'd cradled his head in her lap while she'd called for help, and tried to put pressure on his wounds. He'd stared up into her eyes, his baby blues filled with tears, silently begging her to help him. But he'd been too far gone. He'd died before the ambulance had gotten there, and she'd been left, bathed in his blood, to answer the detectives' questions.

She'd had nothing to tell them. He hadn't said a word, just looked at her, his gaze forever burned into her memory. So, as they'd dug into his murder, she'd followed the case's progress.

She'd learned the kid's name: Simon Mellor. And she'd discovered he was just eighteen years old, a few months out of the foster care system, probably killed running drugs for someone because he couldn't find any better options for himself.

The fury that had filled her then still heated her up whenever she thought about him. The investigation had stalled out and it looked destined to become a cold case, so Brenna had made it her mission to figure out who'd killed the kid. What she'd discovered had led her back to Victor, to the biggest favor she'd ever asked her mentor.

And he'd agreed, gone to their chief and begged for her chance to go undercover in Carlton's operation. Brenna had stood outside the door, just out of sight, but she'd heard her chief's "no way" coming long before he'd said it.

So when he'd announced, "Hartwell could get herself killed," Brenna had pushed open that door, slapped her hands on her hips and told him, "That's a chance I'm willing to take."

This morning, as she slipped into another slinky dress Carlton had bought her, she realized that was a strong possibility. She was way out of her league here. The quick training she'd received on undercover work—how to remember a cover story, how to befriend a criminal and keep the disgust she really felt hidden—could only take her so far. And now, with Marcos here, she felt unfocused when she needed every advantage she could get.

Carlton Wayne White was behind Simon Mellor's death. He hadn't held the knife—he was too far up the chain for something like that. But he'd ordered it. And Brenna was determined to make him pay.

But if that was all there was to it, her chief never would have approved this assignment. What Brenna had uncovered went way deeper than one boy's murder. Because he wasn't the only kid who'd wound up dead shortly after getting out of foster care, with rumors of a drug connection surrounding his murder. She didn't know how he was doing it yet, but Carlton was using the foster care system to find pawns for his crimes.

If she was right, he'd been doing it for years, building his empire on the backs of foster care kids.

Most of what she remembered from that horrible night eighteen years ago was the fire. The smell of the smoke, the feel of it in her lungs. The heat of the blaze, reaching for her, swallowing up everything in its path. But one of the things in its path had been papers, and years later, when she'd seen similar papers at the foster system headquarters, she'd known.

Carlton Wayne White was using someone in the system to get names of kids who were turning eighteen. Kids who'd have nothing: no family, no money, no help. He'd swoop in and offer them a chance to put a roof over their head and food in their bellies. And then they'd die for him.

It all ends soon, she promised herself, yanking open her door and striding into the hallway—and smack into Marcos.

What was he doing outside her room?

She didn't actually have to speak the words, because as he steadied her—yet again—he answered. "Carlton told me to come and get you for breakfast."

She couldn't help herself. Her gaze wandered over him, still hungry for another look after so many years. Today, he was dressed in darkwash jeans and a crewneck sweater that just seemed to emphasize the breadth of his chest.

"Brenna," he said, humor and hunger in his tone.

She looked up, realizing she'd been blatantly ogling him. "Sorry." She flushed.

The hunger didn't fade from his eyes, but his expression grew serious. "Brenna, I want—"

She wanted, too. Maybe it was just the chance to finally do something about her very first crush, or the fact that she'd never expected— but always hoped—to see Marcos again.

It was foolish and wrong for so many reasons, but she couldn't seem to help herself. She leaned up on her tiptoes in another pair of ridiculous shoes and practically fell toward him, looping her arms around his neck.

His hands locked on her waist, and then her lips were on his, just the briefest touch before he set her back on her feet.

"Brenna," he groaned. "We can't do that. Carlton—"

"He's not here right now," she cut him off, not wanting to think about Carlton and the dangerous mission she'd begged to get assigned to. Because all she could think about was Marcos. The boy she'd never been able to forget, morphed into a man she couldn't stop thinking about. She leaned back into him, and she could tell she'd caught him off guard.

Before he could protest again, she fused her lips to his. Just one real taste, she promised herself, and then she'd back away, leave him alone and go back to her mission.

He kissed the way she'd imagined he would

in all those childhood fantasies she'd had, where she grew up and got out of those foster homes she'd been sent to after the fire. Like a fairy-tale ending come to life.

Except this wasn't a fairy tale. And Marcos was a drug dealer.

She pulled away, feeling dazed and unsteady. He didn't look much better; he actually seemed shocked he'd kissed her back at all. But as she stared up at him, breathing hard and trying to pull herself together, she could see it on his face. He was thinking about kissing her again.

And, Lord help her, she wanted him to.

"I warned you to stay away from her!"

Carlton's voice boomed down the hallway, making her jump. She almost fell, but braced herself on the wall as Carlton strode toward them, fury in his expression and ownership in his voice that made a chill run through her.

Then he snapped his fingers and his thugs pounded down the hallway, too.

Marcos put his hands up, trying to placate him, but it didn't matter. One of the guards slung his semiautomatic rifle over his shoulder and punched Marcos in the stomach, making him double over.

As Brenna gasped and yelled for Carlton to

stop them, the thugs each took Marcos by an arm and dragged him down the corridor.

And she knew what was going to happen next. They were going to kill him.

Chapter Four

Marcos tensed his muscles, but it didn't stop the pain when one of Carlton's guards slammed an oversize fist into his stomach. The punch doubled him over, his eyes watering. They'd been hitting him for five minutes, and he could feel it all over his body. Gasping for air, he staggered backward, giving himself a few precious seconds to gauge his options.

Fight or flight?

His car was a few feet behind him, his DEA phone secreted in the hidden compartment, his keys always in his pocket. But there was no way he'd make it. Both bodyguards had semi-automatic weapons slung over their backs. He couldn't run faster than they could swing the weapons around and fire.

Fighting was a problem, too. These two might have looked like more brawn than brain, but they weren't stupid. They were staying on either side of him, one at a time stepping forward for a hit, the other keeping enough distance that he couldn't take on one without the other being able to fire.

Besides, Brenna was still inside. He could hear her, screaming at Carlton to stop them. And it didn't matter what deal she had with the drug kingpin. If Carlton was this angry at Marcos for a simple kiss, what would he do to Brenna for choosing Marcos over him? Marcos couldn't leave her.

Not that he was going to have much of a choice, the way things were going. The guy came at him again, before Marcos could fully recover, and swept his feet out from underneath him.

He hit the concrete hard, pain ricocheting through his skull. Black spots formed in front of his eyes and bile burned his throat. His biggest undercover assignment, and he was going to die all alone in the middle of the Appalachians. Would they even find his body? Would his brothers know what had happened to him?

The thought gave him strength, and as he made out a size thirteen crashing toward him through his wavering vision, Marcos rolled right. His stomach and his head rebelled, but he held it together, shoving himself to his feet. He was unsteady, but standing.

And then he spotted her. Brenna stood in the doorway to the house. She was screaming, he realized—it wasn't just his ears ringing. Carlton had his arms wrapped around her, lifting her off the ground, but not moving as she swung her feet frantically, trying to escape.

Fury lit Marcos, and it seemed to intensify the pain in his head. He must have swayed on his feet, because the guards both moved toward him at once, smiling, and Marcos recognized his chance.

The first guard swung a fist. Instinctively, Marcos ducked, then stepped forward fast, getting close enough to slam an uppercut into his chin.

The guard's head snapped backward, but Marcos didn't waste time with a follow-up punch. He twisted right, bringing his palm up this time, right into the second guard's nose. Blood spurted, spraying Marcos as the guy howled and staggered backward, his hands pressed to his face.

In his peripheral vision, he could see Carlton's surprise as he let Brenna go. She stumbled, losing one of her shoes as she came running toward him. Behind her, Marcos could see Carlton's hand reach behind his back—surely where he had his own weapon.

He opened his mouth to warn Brenna to duck

when the first guy he'd hit shoved himself to his feet. Marcos barreled into him, taking him to the ground hard, his only hope to grab the guy's weapon and shoot first.

It was a desperate move, and unlikely to work, but he didn't even have a chance to try, because the second guy pulled a pistol that had been hidden under his T-shirt. He was swinging it toward Marcos when Brenna slammed into him, taking the guy down despite the fact that he must have outweighed her by a hundred pounds. They fell to the ground together, but Marcos didn't have time to do more than say a silent prayer neither of them had been shot as the guy underneath him suddenly rolled, bucking Marcos off.

He shoved to his knees, ready to slam into the guy again, but he'd somehow managed to yank his AK-47 up toward Marcos.

Marcos's breath caught and then a gunshot rang out.

Shock slammed through him, and it took several seconds before he could process it. He hadn't been hit. The guy in front of him was down, though, eyes staring blankly at the sky, gun lying uselessly at his side.

Marcos glanced over at Carlton, but the man looked as surprised as Marcos felt. Carlton's weapon dangled in his hand, like he'd been getting ready to use it but hadn't been fast enough.

Swiveling to stare at Brenna, Marcos watched as she slowly lowered the weapon she'd somehow gotten away from Carlton's other bodyguard. He lay half underneath her, moaning in pain.

She was breathing hard, blinking rapidly, and he knew instantly that she'd never killed anyone before.

Marcos saw movement from the corner of his eye, and he knew before he looked up that Carlton was raising his gun hand. Marcos gauged the distance to the nearest AK-47, but it was too far, and he knew it even before Carlton barked, "Don't even think about it."

His gaze lifted, and he readied himself for a second time to be shot, but Carlton wasn't pointing the pistol at him.

He was pointing it at Brenna.

"DO YOU HAVE some kind of death wish?"

Carlton's voice, usually loud and boisterous, was scarily quiet. But the menace came through as clearly as if he'd screamed at her as he pointed the gun at her head.

Brenna realized her mistake instantly. She shouldn't have lowered her weapon. She should have swung it toward Carlton.

But she'd never shot anyone before. Sure, she'd fired a weapon hundreds of times. In practice. She'd even held a weapon on resisting suspects before. But she'd never had to use it to protect herself or someone else.

Until now.

There was no question Carlton's bodyguards were going to kill Marcos. Nothing she'd said had swayed the drug lord. And when he'd released her, she'd acted on instinct. Instinct and fury, and something fiercely protective that scared her.

And afterward, when the man had dropped to the ground, no dying scream, no time for surprise to register on his face, her hand had just gone slack on her. She hadn't even consciously decided to kill him and now it was over.

She'd just *killed* someone. Regret hit with the force of a tidal wave, but there hadn't been any other way. She couldn't just stand by and watch Marcos die.

Pushing the emotions down, Brenna tried to focus, telling herself she could deal with her regrets later—assuming she lived through the next few minutes.

"Carlton," Brenna said, her voice shaky. "I was just trying to—"

"You'd die for this man?" Carlton boomed,

making her flinch. "After just a one-night stand?" His eyes narrowed, and he glanced from her to Marcos and back again, but too fast for her to lift her own weapon.

He suspected she and Marcos had a deeper connection than the lie she'd given about picking him up at a bar. And Carlton was right. But she and Marcos had only known each other for a few months. A few months of the worst pain in her life. A pain that had brought her here.

Resolution overtook her fear. She'd come this far. She wasn't going to die without a fight.

And with Carlton, she knew her best weapon wasn't her fists or the gun clutched in her hand. Tossing the pistol away from her, she lifted her hands in the air and got slowly to her feet, stepping slightly away from the bodyguard moaning on the ground.

Her hair was a disaster; pieces of it stuck to her lipstick, more of it was in her eyes. Her knees were skinned and bloody, her dress hiked up way too high. She ignored all of it, locking her gaze on Carlton and tipping her chin up. "You read my file, right? You know about the fire?"

She sensed Marcos tense, but she couldn't dare glance at him as Carlton gave a brief nod.

"Then you must know the rest of it, too." Her voice hitched, remembering the things that had come after that fire, when she'd been sent to other foster homes. Places without smiling boys with dimples to greet her and hold her hand, but older boys with a scary gleam in their eyes.

Carlton's eyes narrowed even more, but she could tell he was listening. Maybe he even cared.

"If you really looked, then you know this isn't about Marcos. Marco," she corrected herself. "It's about me. I'm here because I want a different life from the one I grew up with. I want security. I want to feel safe." She let the truth of those words ring through in her voice. "So, I'll work with you, but you don't own me. If that's what you want, I'm not interested."

A smirk twisted his lips, then faded, and she wasn't sure if she'd just signed her death warrant or gotten through to him.

Beside her, the bodyguard she'd knocked to the ground pulled himself to his knees, snarling at her. For a second, she thought he was going to jump up and tackle her, when Carlton fired his gun, making her jump.

His bodyguard slumped back down, dead.

She stared at Carlton, speechless, and he shrugged. "He failed me. Kind of like you, Brenna."

She hadn't gotten through to him. Brenna took a breath and closed her eyes.

"This is supposed to be a business arrangement, right?" Marcos spoke up.

Brenna opened her eyes again, glancing at him, wondering if it was smart of him to remind Carlton of his presence.

"Because I've got to tell you," Marcos continued, getting to his feet, too, and leaving behind the bodyguard's weapon, which had been at arm's length away, "this is how my family did business. All these feuds. It's derailing their business. Why do you think I want to branch out on my own?"

His family? Brenna frowned, wondering what game he was playing. Some of the kids in the foster homes she'd been to had family out there, either people they'd been taken from because of neglect or abuse, or people who'd given them up. But not Marcos. She knew he'd grown up in the system from the time he was an infant, that they'd never been able to find any extended family. Had that changed? Had he found blood relatives after the fire?

"Let me ask you something, Marco," Carlton replied. "Or is it Marcos?" His gaze snuck to Brenna, then returned. "You've met Brenna once? She was that unforgettable?"

Marcos frowned, and a sick feeling formed in her stomach at the way the drug lord's eyes wandered over her, way more blatantly than he'd ever done before. As if she was his, whether she liked it or not.

Carlton Wayne White was a killer. A man who'd use kids with no one to help them as disposable pawns in his business. Why should it surprise her if he was also a rapist?

She'd been clear with him that she didn't want to sleep with him. She'd thought he actually respected that; she'd believed he saw her as a better business partner because of it. But maybe she'd been fooling herself. Maybe he'd never cared because he hadn't planned to ask.

Before Marcos could answer Carlton's question, he continued, "Or you just have a problem with loyalty? Is that why you're dealing with me instead of sticking with family? I looked into you, Costrales. You're the black sheep, aren't you?"

Marcos shrugged, spitting blood onto the ground. "You say black sheep. I say visionary."

Carlton snorted. "You're awfully confident for a man I still might kill."

"My family and I may not always see eye to eye, but they're pretty good at blood feuds."

Carlton nodded slowly and lowered his weapon. "So they are." He gave a slight smile. "I suppose I don't want to have to deal with your entire family coming after me. Too messy for me to clean up." He nodded at Brenna. "I guess this means you're vouching for her?"

Marcos paused a long moment and Brenna held her breath, not sure what to hope for. Whoever Marcos's family was—if his story was even true—they had sway. But if Marcos vouched for her too quickly, would Carlton really buy that they didn't know one another well? Or would he think the two of them were playing some kind of scam on him, maybe trying to steal away his business?

"I don't really know her," Marcos said, not even glancing her way. "And I don't know what kind of business arrangement you two have. So I'm not sure I can do that. But I'll tell you this much. I betray you? Fine, kill me. I'd do the same. But playing some sort of ownership game with a woman who's not interested and shooting anyone who gets in your way? That's not how I work. So, I tell you what. You leave her alone and so will I."

Carlton tucked his gun back into his waistband and Brenna let out a breath, tugging down her dress and yanking the hair out of her face.

"Well, hasn't the mob gotten progressive?" Carlton asked. "All right. We've got a deal." He glanced at Brenna. "I guess this means our time together is over."

He turned and walked inside, and Brenna

stood rooted in place. That was it? All the months of work and she'd let a foolish attraction to a man she hadn't seen in almost two decades ruin everything?

She blinked back tears as Marcos sent her a brief, unreadable glance and followed Carlton, leaving her all alone in the drug lord's driveway.

Chapter Five

When she'd joined the police department, Brenna had known the day might come where she'd have to shoot someone in the line of duty. It was a responsibility she'd accepted, the idea that she might have to take one life to save another.

But nothing could have prepared her for the roll of emotions making her chest feel tight and her stomach churn right now. She pressed a hand to her stomach and tried to calm her breathing as she stood just inside Carlton's mansion.

His two remaining guards had been called up and were dealing with the bodies outside, and then they were supposed to escort her to her car and send her home. But after all the work she'd put in to get here, she couldn't leave. Not like this. Not with Carlton still planning business deals, and Simon Mellor with no one else willing to take up his cause.

The truth was, there were a lot of Simon Mellors out there. Other kids just like him who were getting ready to leave the foster system and had no idea the challenges that awaited them. Kids who Carlton might target by offering them things they couldn't resist, like a way not to be homeless and hungry.

Brenna straightened and strode to her room. She yanked off the dress, heels and diamonds Carlton had been trying to woo her with, and she'd been pretending to be infatuated with, and traded them for her normal clothes. Then she headed to the living room, where Carlton had settled alone after killing one of his own guards. She might have thought he felt some regret, too, but she didn't think the man knew what that meant.

Throwing the clothes and jewelry at him, she planted her hands on her hips and exclaimed, "I thought you were a businessman!"

He shoved the items off him onto the floor and raised an eyebrow. "And I didn't realize that you were a drama queen."

"I came here because of all the things we talked about over the past few months. I came here to start a business deal with you, and this is what you do to me?"

"Careful now," he said, the amusement dropping off his face. "I gave you a second chance today. Don't make me regret it."

"How is this a second chance? Sending me home with nothing?"

"I'm letting you live, aren't I?"

His words stalled her angry tirade, but she shouldn't have been surprised. She hadn't had enough of a plan when she'd come out here.

Taking a deep breath, Brenna started over. "Look, we each have something the other one wants. You plan to find someone else in the foster care system who can do this for you? Fine, give it your best shot. Most of them are overworked and underpaid and are either there because it's what they can get, or because they want to make a difference. You approach the first type and yeah, you might get a bite, but they won't be as aggressive about this as I will. You approach the second type, and you'll get turned in to the police so fast your head will spin."

"The police," Carlton mocked. "They're not smart enough to prove anything."

But she could see on his face that her words were getting through to him, that he wanted her connections more than he was showing, so she pressed on. "I started working in the system because I thought maybe I could make things better for kids like me. But the truth is, that will never happen. Someone like *you* is their best chance. And you're mine, too, because I might not have had control over my life since I was thrown into the system, but I do now. And I plan to make the most of it."

A slow smile spread over Carlton's face. "I may have acted too hastily, Brenna. Consider your invitation to stay here extended, and our business deal back on." He looked her over, from her well-used tennis shoes to her inexpensive T-shirt. "But before I hand over any more benefits like diamonds and clothes, you're going to have to prove yourself."

She nodded, elation and disgust with herself at the tactics she was using fighting for control. In the end, determination won out. Before this weekend was over, she was going to have Carlton on the hook with a plan he couldn't resist.

And that would be the beginning of his downfall.

"What are you doing here?" Marcos had been sitting on a bench outside, but he lurched to his feet, nearly groaning aloud at the pain that spiked all over his body. He almost thought the hits he'd taken to the head were giving him hallucinations.

But there was no way even his mind could

conjure up Brenna like this. She looked antsy in a pair of jeans and a loose aqua T-shirt that made her brown skin seem to glow and brought out the caramel highlights in her hair. Instead of the stilettos she'd been wearing all weekend, she wore a pair of hot pink gym shoes. The outfit looked way more natural on her than the skintight dresses and ridiculous heels.

She was also teary-eyed as she looked him over, her gaze lingering on his myriad of bruises that had turned a dark purple since this morning. But she didn't say a word about them, just took a deep breath.

He'd expected her to be long gone by now. And he'd been equal parts relieved and depressed over it all morning.

"I convinced Carlton that we should still be working together."

A million dark thoughts ran through Marcos's mind as he lowered himself carefully back onto the bench. "How?"

"Carlton might have a bad temper—and apparently a possessive streak—but at heart, he's a businessman."

Marcos felt himself scowl and tried to hide it. A real drug dealer would think of himself as a businessman, not a criminal.

By the expression on her face, she'd seen it, but she didn't say anything, just continued, "I have access that he wants. And he's better off with someone who will do the job without a personal distraction."

He held in the slew of swear words that wanted to escape and instead asked calmly, "You sure it's a good idea after what happened today?"

"No." She let out a humorless laugh and sank onto the bench across from him. "But I've come too far to give up now."

What did that mean? He suddenly realized he'd been so distracted by seeing her again that he'd failed to dig into why she was here. He knew what Carlton could offer Brenna: money. But what could she offer him, especially now that she'd made it clear sex was off the table? She said she worked in the foster care system, not exactly the sort of connection Carlton would need.

"What exactly is your arrangement with Carlton?" Marcos asked.

She fidgeted, as though she'd been hoping to avoid this question. "I can get him information he needs."

The answer was purposely vague and Marcos raised an eyebrow.

"How about you, Marc-O?" she pressed. "What can you give him?"

"A new network," Marcos answered simply,

wishing he didn't have to lie to her. Wishing it didn't come so easily. But that was good—it meant all his training had worked if he could even lie to Brenna.

"For drugs? How?"

It was time to get off this topic and convince Brenna to rethink her decision to stay here. "Carlton is dangerous," Marcos said softly.

"Yeah, no kidding," she replied, looking him over again.

Her voice cracked as she asked, "How badly are you hurt?"

"Could have been worse. Thank you for that. Where'd you learn to fight?"

Her legs jiggled a little, a clear sign he was about to get less than the full truth. "Foster care." She glanced around, then lowered her voice. "Not all of us can find long-lost family."

"Yeah, well…" Now it was his turn to feel antsy, but he'd had a lot of practice being undercover. So why did lying to her feel so wrong? "Carlton doesn't know about my years in foster care, and I'd like to keep it that way."

She tipped her head, like she was waiting for more details, but he stayed silent. Better if she just kept her mouth shut about his past altogether. Because the story Carlton knew didn't match up with Marcos *ever* having been in foster care.

As far as Carlton knew, he'd grown up in the massive Costrales family, where joining organized crime was in the blood. The DEA had backstopped a story for him that involved being a bit estranged from his family, but still on the payroll. As far as they could tell, Carlton's empire didn't yet stretch to the area the Costrales family ran, but there was no way to prepare for all possible overlap.

On paper, Marco Costrales was the youngest son of Bennie Costrales, born of a mistress. He hadn't grown up with the Costrales name, but he'd been given it—and a large sum of money to build his own empire—when he'd hit eighteen. On paper, Marco had gone to jail a few times, but never for anything major. Just enough to show he was in deep to something the Feds couldn't prove.

It was their best way in, because years of trying to infiltrate Carlton's organization had proved he wasn't willing to work with anyone he didn't know. This was the DEA's way of upping the ante, because they knew Carlton had always wanted to expand his connections. The problem was, if Carlton had a personal connection to the Costrales family they didn't know about and he asked about Marco, he'd quickly find there was no such person.

And then today's beating would look like

a party in comparison to what would happen to Marcos.

"How are Cole and Andre?" Brenna asked, bringing him back to the present. "The three of you are still family, too, I assume? Even after your biological family came into the picture?"

Was that wistfulness in her voice? Had she never found anyone to call family in all her years in the system?

He knew it happened. He'd bounced around from one foster home to the next from birth until he was seven. Then he'd landed in the foster home with Cole Walker and Andre Diaz, and for the first time in his life, he'd realized how little blood mattered. These were the brothers of his heart. Five years later, when their house had burned down, they'd been split up until each of them had turned eighteen. And now they lived within an hour of one another and saw each other all the time. The way real brothers would.

"They're doing good. Both are getting married in the next year." He didn't mention their profession, because how could he explain being a drug dealer if he told her Cole was a police detective and Andre an FBI agent?

"Did they ever put you back together?" She twisted her hands together, like she knew she was getting into dangerous territory.

"You mean after you set the house on fire?"

She flushed. "I didn't know you realized... I was young. It was stupid."

"Why was our foster father in the back of the house with you when that fire started?" It was something he'd been wondering—and dreading finding the answer to—for months. He'd never expected to be able to ask Brenna herself.

"What?"

Brenna's eyes widened, and she had to be wondering how he'd known that when he shouldn't have even known she'd set the fire in the first place. At the time, all the reports on the fire had called it an accident. Only recently had he seen an unsealed juvenile record showing that Brenna had set the fire. But it had been his brother who'd remembered that neither Brenna nor their foster father had been where they should have been when the fire started.

The rest of the family had been upstairs in bed, asleep. So why had Brenna and their foster father been downstairs, in the back of the house, in his study?

"How did you know that?"

"Was he hurting you?" Marcos's chest actually hurt as he waited for the answer.

She shook her head. "No. It was...look, he found me in his office. I'd lit the candle, and he came in and I tossed it."

Why was he positive she was lying? "I don't believe you."

She looked ready to run away on those more sensible shoes. "Why not? You said you knew I'd set the fire."

Marcos leaned back, studying her, wondering why she'd lie about the reasons for setting the fire, the reasons for his foster father being nearby, when she so easily admitted to setting it. His agent instincts were going crazy, but he wasn't sure about what. "I meant, I didn't believe you about why he was there." There was way more here than he'd ever realized. "I think you owe me the truth."

"You, Cole and Andre were reunited, right? What does it matter now? I was upset about my mom's death. I—"

"I almost didn't make it out of that house." The fact was, it was amazing none of them had died in there that day.

She sucked in an audible gasp.

Those moments after he'd dived through the living-room window came back to him, Cole slamming into him, knocking him to the ground and patting out the fire that had caught the back of his pajamas. He remembered Brenna running around the side of the house a minute later, just as the ambulance doors had closed. He didn't think she'd seen him, but it was the last memory he had of that day.

Brenna's terrified face, their house burning to the ground behind her.

"STAY HERE!"

Her foster father's voice rang in her ears now as clearly as if he was sitting right beside her, as clearly as if it was eighteen years ago. But back then, she couldn't have moved if she'd tried.

She'd been dry heaving into the grass, her lungs burning from all the smoke, her eyes swollen almost shut. The fire had caught fast. She wouldn't have made it out of there at all if he hadn't screamed at her, then yanked her right off her feet and ran for the back door.

He'd practically flung her on the grass, then turned back, surely to return for his wife and the other foster kids in the house. But the door they'd come through had been engulfed by then. She'd watched through watery eyes as he'd tried to break a window, searched for another way in. She didn't know how long he'd contemplated, before he took off running for the front of the house.

She'd picked herself off the ground and limped after him and relief had overtaken her. Their foster mother was clutching two of the foster kids close. Three more were huddled together closer to the house. Only—

No, it wasn't three. It was two, with a paramedic tending to one of them.

Panic had started anew because Marcos had been missing. Then she'd seen the ambulance as it flew away from the house. She'd started screaming then, and hadn't stopped until someone had told her over and over again that Marcos was okay.

Within hours, she'd been at the hospital herself, getting checked out, then hustled off to a new foster home. She'd never seen anyone from that house again. The truth was, she'd never expected to.

"I saw the ambulance," she told Marcos now. "But they told me you were okay, that it was just a precaution."

She must have looked panicked, because he got up and sat beside her, taking her hand in his. And it should have felt very, very wrong so close to Carlton's house, after what had just happened, but instead it felt right. Her fingers curled into his.

"I'm okay. But I spent years wondering what bad luck it was that I'd finally found my family, only to have them torn away from me."

Tears pricked the backs of her eyes. She knew exactly how that felt, only in a different order. All her life, it had just been her and her mom. They'd been more than family; they'd been best friends, the two of them against the world. And then one drunk driver, one slippery patch of road, had taken her whole life away.

"At least you got them back," she whispered, even though she knew it was an unfair thing to say. It wasn't his fault her mom had died. And it wasn't his fault he believed she was to blame for splitting up him and his brothers. She'd told him as much.

"I did, eventually," he said softly. "What about you? You never found anyone to call family after you left that house? I'd always hoped you would."

Her hand tightened instinctively in his. She didn't like to think about those days. They were long gone now. "No."

"And what you were telling Carlton, about why you wouldn't sleep with him? About your file? You want to tell me about that?"

His voice was softer, wary, like he was afraid what she might say, and she hesitated. It was in her file in the foster system, because back then, she'd been stupid enough to think that if she could just get out of that house, the next one would be okay. Maybe it would be like the one with Marcos. Maybe they'd even move her wherever they'd sent Marcos. But they hadn't. And she'd learned to take care of herself.

She was going to shake her head, but when she glanced at him, she realized if she didn't tell him, he'd think the worst. And somehow, even after believing she'd purposely set fire to their house and almost killed him, he still cared what had happened to her.

"The place I was sent to next, there were two older boys who lived there. One was in foster care, like me. The other was the foster parents' son. The first night I was there, they came into my room, and they told me they owned me now."

Marcos didn't say anything, but his jaw tightened. "You were eleven."

"Yeah. Not all foster homes were like the one we were in." As she said it, she realized the irony. In his mind, she'd been the one to destroy that.

But all he said was, "I know."

"It was bad." She glossed through the rest of it. "They came after me, and I got lucky. And after that, I learned how to fight. That's what you saw today."

A shiver went through her at the memory. Those boys had been fifteen and sixteen, and much bigger than her. They'd come toward her, and she'd screamed her head off. One of them had tried to smother her with a pillow while the other yanked at her clothes. She'd expected her new foster parents to come running into the room, because she knew they were home, but they hadn't. Luck had been on her side, though, because police officers happened to be on a traffic stop down the street and heard her screaming.

She'd told the cops what had happened, she'd told the foster care workers what had happened, and instead of looking as horrified as she'd felt, they'd looked resigned. They'd moved her to a new foster home, and the first thing she'd done was to steal a steak knife and hide it under her pillow. That year, she'd stolen money from those foster parents to pay off some older kids at school to teach her to fight.

"And now?" he asked. "You didn't find family growing up, but what about afterward? You must have a circle of friends, a boyfriend?"

She shrugged. "Sure. Not a boyfriend," she added quickly, though it would probably be better for both of them if he thought she did. "But friends, sure." Sort of. She only let them get so close, though. Foster care had taught her how quickly people came and went, and it was usually easier to keep them at a distance.

"Are you sure this is the direction you want

to go? Working with Carlton? There's still time to back out."

She shook her head. "No, there's not. He and I have a deal. And I might not be totally convinced he won't turn on me anyway, but I know one thing for sure. If I back out now, he *will* kill me."

Chapter Six

Brenna looked around the garden. It was late November, and what had apparently been a flower garden was now bare vines and plants. Around them, fir trees rose a hundred feet in the air, mixed with trees in various stages of losing their leaves. Everything was orange and red, and it reminded her of fire.

It reminded her of *the* fire. She wanted desperately to tell Marcos the truth, but that would blow her cover. And even though she couldn't reconcile the sweet boy with the huge dimples with the mob-connected man jumping into the drug business, she needed to remember he was a criminal. But *how* had he ended up with a mafia family?

"I thought you were Greek," she blurted.

"Yeah, well, apparently I got renamed when I entered the system," Marcos said as he pulled his hand free and stood. "My biological family tracked me down later. I went to live with my mom, and then my dad came into the picture, got me connected."

It made sense, and she knew it happened—people who'd lost their kids to the system reconnecting years later. So why did she feel like he was making up this story on the fly? Surely Carlton would know if he wasn't part of a Mafia family.

But he was backing away from her slowly, and she knew whatever his story, asking about it was driving him away. And he might be her best bet for information right now.

"Have you met any of Carlton's other business partners?" It wasn't her best segue, but he stopped moving.

"Not really. Just his nephew. That's how I got invited."

"His nephew." Brenna nodded, disappointed. She knew Jesse, too, and she felt sorry for the kid. Fact was, she felt a bit of a kinship with him. His family died, and he got thrown in with Carlton. What choice had the kid really had? Probably fall in line with Carlton or get tossed into the cold—or worse.

Anger heated her, the reminder of why she was here. It wasn't about Marcos Costa. It was about Simon Mellor, the eighteen-year-old boy who'd died in her arms.

"So you haven't seen Carlton with kids?"

"Kids?" Marcos frowned. "What do you mean?"

"Eighteen, nineteen. Kids who work for him?" The words poured out, even though she knew she was stepping in dangerous territory. If she wasn't careful, she was going to sound like a cop interrogating a suspect. Her heart rate picked up as he continued to stare at her, those gorgeous blue-gray eyes narrowed.

"I've never met Carlton before yesterday," Marcos said slowly.

She held in a curse. She should have realized this was a first meeting. She'd just assumed they'd had others and that this weekend was a final test.

"Why do you want to know about kids who work for Carlton? And what exactly do you think they do for him?"

She tried to look nonchalant, even though her blood pressure had to be going crazy right now. "I'm just trying to figure out how his business works, what I'm getting into here."

He wasn't buying it. He didn't have to say a word for her to know she'd made him suspicious.

"What are you getting into, Brenna? You never did tell me exactly what kind of access you could offer Carlton."

In this moment, all the years they hadn't seen each other didn't matter. The fact that he was an aspiring drug lord with mob connections didn't matter. Because she knew without a doubt that if he figured out what she was pretending to do, he'd hate her. And he'd do whatever he could to stop her from working with Carlton.

He'd been in the system since he was an infant. And even at twelve years old, he'd talked to her about the plans he and his brothers had— plans to look out for one another when they left the system. He'd known there was no net for foster care kids. And the fact that she was pretending to take advantage of that would be a worse sin than anything he was doing.

"You work in the foster care system," he said before she could come up with a believable lie. "You said you wanted to start a program to help kids make the transition to the real world." He shook his head, looking disgusted. "What does that mean, really? Carlton sets up front businesses and you populate them with foster kids to do his dirty work?"

"I…" She faltered, trying to figure out how to smooth this over without risking him hearing the truth from Carlton anyway.

Then his eyes narrowed, and he took a step closer until she was forced to lean back to look at him. "What aren't you telling me, Brenna? Why are you really here?"

"You're a cop, aren't you?"

It made total sense, Marcos realized, instantly relieved. Except if a police department was running an operation on Carlton, the DEA would know about it. Anything to do with drug operations by any organization went into a system the DEA could access. And they'd made very sure before he came here. There was nothing.

She stared at him, her lips parted like she wanted to say something but couldn't figure out what, silently shaking her head. There was panic in her eyes.

But was it because he'd uncovered the truth? Or because she was afraid he'd peg her as a cop when she wasn't and Carlton would kill her for it?

As much as he wanted to believe she was here with noble intentions, the truth was that his judgment was compromised when it came to Brenna. His feelings for her were all tangled up in the past, in the first girl who'd ever made his heart beat faster. In the fantasies he'd had growing up, of one day seeing her again. The fact was, he'd never really given up on those dreams.

"No." She'd finally found her voice. "Why would you think that? Anyway, you really think a police department would hire someone who'd set a house on fire?"

"Probably depends on the department and the circumstances of that fire," he replied evenly, still studying her. She was flushed, nervous. If she was a cop, she had limited experience undercover—and what police department would send a rookie into an operation like Carlton Wayne White's? Still, his instincts were buzzing, telling him something here wasn't as it seemed. "That record just got unsealed. Why?"

"You saw it."

It wasn't a question, but it probably should have been, because there weren't a lot of reasons a criminal would have been able to access that record. He silently cursed himself. If he wasn't careful, Brenna's mere presence was going to make him blow his own cover.

"Yeah, I saw it." And it hadn't occurred to him before—why was it unsealed all of a sudden? "It was a trap," he realized. "A way to backstop you as a foster care worker with the right motivations to work with him, but that easily fit into your actual identity. Someone who had criminal actions in her past. And you must be new, if there's no easy way to track you as a cop. So, what department do you work for?"

"Stop saying that!" She jumped up, jammed her hands on her hips and got in his face, despite being a solid five inches shorter than he was. "If I'm a cop, then you're—" She went pale and swayed, then whispered, "No way. You're…what? DEA?"

He smirked at her, though inside his brain was screaming at him. "Don't try to turn this around on me."

Brenna took a few steps backward, still staring at him contemplatively. What she was trying to decide was written all over her face: could she trust him?

And that told him everything he needed to know.

He swore, harshly enough that she flinched in surprise. "You're going to get yourself killed," he snapped at her. "How many undercover operations have you run? You shouldn't even play poker!"

"Hey!" she snapped back. "Don't be a jerk! I'm not a cop, and I don't know what you're trying to—"

"You're right," he told her, breaking every rule in undercover work. "The mob story was backstopping, okay? I'm DEA."

Her lips parted and relief flashed in her

eyes, followed by uncertainty. "Is this some kind of—"

"I'm not trying to trick you. You think I'd risk my life for that?"

"And it's perfectly safe to tell a criminal that you're an undercover agent?"

Marcos smiled. "It is when the criminal I'm telling is really a cop. Let's work together. We're after Carlton for pretty obvious reasons—he's got control of a big chunk of the heroin supply. What about you? Because if it was drugs, it should have been put in the system so exactly this didn't happen."

He held his breath as she stayed silent, clearly torn. He was pretty sure he was right, but if not…

"Yes, I'm a police officer. Out of West Virginia. And you're right, it's not in your system because this isn't about drugs. I'm after him for murder."

There was a long silence as they stared at each other. She looked as relieved as he felt, but he couldn't say exactly why. Probably because she had some form of backup now. His relief should have been the same, but the truth was, he was used to going into meets with drug dealers by himself. Maybe not for so long or this far from help, but it was a normal part of the job. And besides, it was clear she was a rookie, at least when it came to undercover work. No, his relief was all about Brenna the woman.

The fact that she wasn't using the foster care system to lure newly released kids to Carlton meant he didn't need to feel guilty that the attraction he'd felt for her as a kid wasn't gone. Not even close. Because even when he'd believed she was here for no good, he'd been drawn to her.

But maybe that guilt was a good thing, because now keeping his distance was going to be a real challenge.

"Just remember Carlton will kill you."

"What?" Brenna squeaked.

"Sorry." He couldn't believe he'd said that out loud. He'd meant it as an internal warning to himself. Maybe the hits to his head really had impacted his judgment. "Just be careful," he amended.

She sank back to the bench. "So what now?"

"Well, you know pretty much all there is to know about why the DEA is after Carlton—we have been for years, and it's straightforward. He's a drug dealer, and we want him gone. I want your story."

She glanced around, reminding him that despite being several hundred feet from the house, with no good way to sneak up without being seen, they were still on Carlton's property.

"You're right about me being a rookie, and you're right that it's the reason I'm using my real name. They scrubbed me from the police records anyway, but there wasn't much, and my department isn't big on putting our faces on a website, thank goodness. So it worked out when I brought them this plan to come in and play to Carlton's weakness."

"What's that? Beautiful women?"

Her cheeks went deep red. "Thanks, but no." She locked her hands together. "Six months ago, I was on foot patrol when a kid died in my arms. He was eighteen, barely out of foster care. And he was running drugs for Carlton."

Marcos nodded slowly. He understood that sort of motivation for pushing an undercover op, but her superiors were doing her a disservice by letting her follow through, with what had to be minimal training and experience. "So, you're here trying to prove Carlton ordered the hit? Because he's careful. I don't think—"

"Not exactly. What you guessed about what I was offering him is right. But I'm not the first one to do it."

Marcos leaned forward, grimacing as his entire left side protested. "Who?"

"I don't know. But I think Carlton has been using foster care kids just out of the system for a long time."

"We haven't seen evidence of that," Marcos said slowly. And yet, it made sense. The DEA's method when grabbing a low-level dealer was usually to try to flip the person to go higher. But with Carlton, that hadn't worked because no one had ever flipped on him, so they couldn't identify who his dealers were. Foster kids with no one in the world except a man who'd given them a roof and a job wouldn't turn on him. And if they'd tried, Marcos was pretty sure Carlton had gotten to them before they could get to the police.

He swore. "How did you get wind of this? The kid talked to you before he died?"

"No. And his case went cold. But I followed the progress. I looked into his life, saw some evidence that he'd approached the station a few times, indicating he might have some information on a dealer. But he never gave it up, so no file was opened. Eventually I tracked down an address he shared with a couple other kids, also out of the system. They wouldn't talk to me. But as I was leaving, I saw him. Carlton. And I knew. I mean, what better drug runners than kids coming out of foster care with no home, no money, no family? And who's going to push for answers if they get killed?"

Marcos nodded slowly. It was flimsy, so flimsy most departments wouldn't have even

let her pursue it as a case, let alone an undercover operation. But he'd been doing this a long
time, and he could feel it. She was right.

"There's more," Brenna said, taking his hand
in both of hers.

He squeezed back, momentarily distracted
by the softness of her skin. It was deceiving,
because he'd seen her take down a man almost
twice her size.

"The fire—"

"I know. The juvenile file was faked, right?
You didn't set the fire." He prayed she was
going to confirm it, but from the look on her
face, he wasn't going to like her answer.

"No, I didn't set it. My department faked
the file. We wanted to blend my real past with
something that would make me seem as though
I could be paid off. But I saw our foster father
set the fire."

Marcos tried to line that up with what he remembered. "Why? He burned down his own
house, risked all of our lives, his wife's life?"

"It wasn't on purpose. I don't think he expected me to be awake. I startled him when I
came into his office—I was confused. I hadn't
been in the house long, and I was practically
sleepwalking, used to the layout of my mom's
house." She let out a breath. "I'd been headed
to the kitchen for a drink. But then he spotted

me and jumped up. He knocked over a candle on his desk. He had so many papers, spread out all over it. The fire caught really fast. At first, he tried to put it out, but it jumped, and then he grabbed me and ran."

"It was an accident." All those years, the original accounts had been right—sort of. They'd assumed everyone had gone to sleep and someone had left a candle burning. But it was still an accident. A simple mistake that had cost him the presence of his brothers for six years. And Brenna.

"Yes, but the papers, Marcos. I saw them as we were trying to get out. I didn't put it together for years, but then I had to go to the foster system headquarters when I was trying to track down Simon—the kid who died—any family he might have had. I saw similar papers."

"Our foster dad was just fostering kids. He didn't work for them," Marcos said, confused. "Are you sure—"

"Yeah, I'm sure. That night is burned in my mind. He shouldn't have had those papers, and I don't know how he got them, but they weren't on us. There were other names on them. I couldn't tell you the names, but I know this much—"

"You think he was Carlton's connection, eighteen years ago?"

"Yes. I looked into it and from what I can tell, Carlton was just getting started then."

"And he built an empire on the backs of foster kids," Marcos said darkly.

He'd wanted to bring down Carlton before, but now that desire intensified until it became a smoldering hate in his gut. If this man held the truth to why he'd spent six years being tossed from home to home, always hoping to see Cole and Andre again, Marcos was going to get it. No matter what it took.

Chapter Seven

Dinner was uncomfortable.

Brenna kept her attention on her plate as she picked at her food. Across from her, Carlton's nephew Jesse did the same, clearly sensing the tension even though he'd managed to miss the beating and screaming and gunshots that afternoon. Apparently, he'd been in the basement, in Carlton's personal soundproofed gun range. Beside her, she felt Carlton's presence like a tornado on the horizon.

She'd been avoiding looking at Marcos all night. He sat on her other side, and he almost made her more nervous than Carlton, though for a completely different reason. DEA. Two days ago, if she'd been asked to guess what Marcos Costa was doing these days, neither mob-connected drug dealer nor DEA agent would have made the list. But it fit.

Now that she thought about it, it wouldn't

surprise her if both of his brothers had gone into law enforcement, too. They'd been so different in the foster home: Cole, the oldest, reliable and even-tempered, the one everyone turned to if they needed something. Andre, the middle of the three, easygoing, but with intensity in his gaze, quick to stand by his brothers. And Marcos, the youngest, who could be quietly watchful or funny and gregarious, depending on his mood. But they'd had a core goodness to them that had her sticking close when she'd found herself all alone. And they hadn't let her down back then. They'd stood up for her, too, when she needed them.

She could imagine them all still living by that motto: helping people, defending people. Joining the police force was something that had ultimately pulled her back in, partly because she'd thought if she could return to her eleven-year-old self and tell Marcos, Cole and Andre she wanted to be a cop, they would have been proud.

"Don't be so glum," Carlton boomed, making Brenna jump in her seat. "Just because I tried to have you killed isn't a reason not to enjoy your filet."

He grinned, and Brenna was struck again by how much of a caricature he seemed, in his standard all-white suit with that white-blond hair brushing his shoulders. He probably had to have the suits specially made, given his size. He might have been in his midforties, but he looked a decade younger, probably from all the hours he spent in a gym. But it wasn't his size that made Brenna nervous. It was the contrast between his usually jolly nature and his quick temper.

Even without his two primary bodyguards, Carlton was still surrounded by protection. His chef—whom Carlton had apparently lured away from a five-star restaurant—was also a mixed martial artist who carried a Glock on his hip and constantly had a sharp knife in his hand. Another pair of guards had quickly taken the place of the first two, though she had no idea if they'd driven in or had been here the whole time. And then there was Jesse, who looked as nervous as she felt, but still reached instinctively for his gun whenever there was a loud noise.

"Don't worry about that," Marcos replied evenly, sounding like a seasoned dealer—or a really practiced undercover agent. "I won't take it personally unless you try it again."

Carlton guffawed. "Don't cross me and it won't be a problem. I'll make you rich."

Brenna glanced at Marcos as he smiled and took a bite of steak. "That's why I'm here."

Carlton tapped her hand, and Brenna resisted the urge to yank it away. "I'd planned to take you down to my gun range and teach you to shoot tonight, but since it appears you already know your way around a gun, perhaps we can talk business."

Her pulse picked up and she nodded.

Carlton slowly rubbed his fingers over her hand. "Who taught you to shoot, by the way?"

She pulled her hand free. "I taught myself. A couple hundred hours at a gun range, and you eventually pick it up."

"But today was the first time you killed anyone, wasn't it?" he pressed.

She looked him in the eyes. "Yes."

"And how did it feel?"

"What?"

Carlton leaned closer, a smile playing on one side of his mouth. "There's nothing like the power of choosing life and death, is there?"

She held back the shiver, but she didn't think it mattered—he'd seen it in her gaze. "That's not really my idea of fun," she said, her voice shaky. "I'd prefer to stick to paperwork."

Carlton leaned back, and she could see on his face that he'd gotten what he'd wanted from her. But what exactly that was, she couldn't tell.

"Do enough paperwork and the diamonds I let you wear earlier can be yours to keep."

She nodded, setting down her fork. "That's why I'm here. But as much as I love jewelry, I'd like to know how to turn it into cash without anyone being the wiser."

Carlton snorted. "You're looking for a tutorial from me on how to hide money?"

She shrugged. "You're going to pay me for a job. Obviously you don't want anyone to notice my new funds. And neither do I. What I want is a nest egg, so that I never have to rely on anyone ever again."

"I knew there was a reason I'd picked you," Carlton said, and Brenna could practically feel Marcos hiding a smile beside her.

Marcos had been right about her minimal training for undercover work. The fact was, this was her first undercover assignment. But the reason they'd gone with her real name was so she could stick as close to the truth as possible. Her trainer had told her to take her real emotions and channel them a different way— if she hadn't chosen law enforcement, if morals weren't an issue, what would matter to her most?

This kind of fiction was easy to remember, but it sure played havoc on her mental state. Because safety and security really *were* two of her life goals. She lived minimally, socking away her savings so that she'd always have a safety net. She relied only on herself, because that way she wouldn't be let down.

How different was she from the character she was pretending to be? And if Carlton found out the truth—or turned on her again at random—and she died out here, what would she be leaving behind?

It terrified her that the answer might be nothing.

THE MEETING WITH Carlton had been a bust.

Sure, he'd given her a rundown on a million different ways to hide money from authorities—some she'd never seen before, even on the other side of the law. But whenever she tried to broach details on next steps with the foster system, he'd pushed her off, telling her they'd get to that later.

This had always been a long-term plan. No one at her police station who knew about the operation—which were very few, to avoid potential leaks—thought they'd get enough on Carlton over just one weekend. Talk had been of her keeping up her cover at the foster care system for months, maybe even years.

But she just had one more day to go at Carlton's hidden mansion, and already she was itching to return to her normal life, to take a dozen showers and wash off the filth she felt being surrounded by this much evil. And she wasn't sure she could wait a year to nail him for Simon's death. How many more boys and girls would die in that year?

Which was why, once Carlton had given her a lingering kiss on the cheek, shooed her out the door of his office and called Marcos in, she hadn't headed to her room to sleep. Instead, she was walking down the long hallway toward where she suspected Carlton slept and trying to look natural. Because though he might have been down two guards, he had two more who seemed anxious to prove themselves. And they eyed her with suspicion and distrust.

Besides, she knew it wouldn't take much to push Carlton back over the edge.

She shot one more glance at the ceiling, on careful watch for any cameras, and then slipped into the room she'd seen Carlton enter last night after he thought she was asleep. Blinking in the darkness, she let her eyes adjust and then gasped. This wasn't Carlton's bedroom. She'd just hit the jackpot. This was a second office.

Rushing over to the massive desk dominating the center of the room, Brenna almost tripped on a bear rug that looked real. She tried not to think about the poor creature who'd given his life to be walked on and went for the top drawer of the desk, heart pounding. It was locked.

She tried the rest of them, but they were all locked. There was no key in any of the obvious hiding spots and no papers lying on his desk. She swore under her breath, then hurried to the filing cabinet, with the same luck. It figured he'd be careful—if rumors were right, he'd been in the drug business for twenty years, and he'd never done hard time.

She might be able to pick the locks, but it would take her a while, and every second she spent in here could be the difference between making it back to her room safely or being dragged outside and shot. Still, she couldn't leave with nothing.

Then, she spotted it. The pad of paper on his desk was blank, but maybe... She ran back over there, happy to be in her regular gym shoes instead of those embarrassingly unsteady heels. She ran her fingers over the top sheet, and her pulse picked up for a new reason. Indentations.

Rather than trying to figure them out, she just ripped the page off and shoved it in her pocket. She was reaching for the door handle when the door opened, almost slamming into her. Brenna jerked backward, out of the way, but there was no time to hide.

She braced herself for Carlton's wrath.

CARLTON WAYNE WHITE'S office was dressed in all white, just like him. It was an odd room, with a huge white desk that actually made Carlton look normal-size, and all white cabinets behind him. There was a framed blueprint of his mansion on the wall, the design signed by Carlton himself. Apparently the man had other hobbies besides watching his thugs beat up disobedient would-be business partners.

Marcos sat on the other side of the desk, feeling like he'd wandered into the twilight zone. This didn't feel like a drug lord's office. Then again, most of his meetings were with dealers out on the streets. They did business out of the back of a car, a hotel room or a fast-food joint. On the rare but wonderful occasions he got to arrest a big player, it still didn't tend to be in an office like this.

He'd done deals on luxury yachts, in luxury homes and in opulent clubs. But never in an office that looked like it could belong to an obsessive-compulsive architect.

"I thought we said no business this weekend," Carlton reminded him as Marcos pressed for the third time about details.

So far, the meeting in Carlton's office had been nothing but a test, Carlton asking questions about Marcos to make sure his story was consistent. Given the stakes—his life—Marcos should have been nervous. But he trusted his training, and so far, he hadn't stumbled once. And he was getting tired of the third degree.

"And I thought I'd come here for a deal, not a beating and the runaround," Marcos replied, staying casual with his legs crossed in front of him while he slouched in the chair. The attitude of a man who'd grown up with a crime family guaranteeing power and money, but where danger was common, too. The real Costrales family had been known to take out their own for any kind of betrayal.

Carlton practically snarled as he leaned toward Marcos across the enormous desk. "I'd advise you to watch your tone."

"Look," Marcos said, straightening in his chair, "if you want to play games, fine, but I'm giving up a weekend for this. And I don't give up a weekend for anyone. Time is money, my friend, and if it's not going to be yours, it'll be someone else's. Now, I think you and I can build a great partnership here, but considering that you set your goons loose on me and I didn't walk, I'd like a little good faith in return."

Carlton stared at him a long minute and then nodded. "Fair enough. You've got balls, Costrales, and you'll need them in this business.

But this vetting process isn't over, so I tell you what. You get one question."

One question. Marcos knew he should ask about distribution or sources, something they could use to find a leak in the organization if this operation didn't go as planned. But instead, he found himself asking, "If you and I go into business together, what guarantees do I have that nothing will come back to me?"

Not giving Carlton a chance to answer, he continued, "Because from what I can tell, what usually does people in with this sort of *business*," he said, grinning, "are the low-level dealers. It's why I've avoided getting involved before, despite the obvious cash flow. But your business intrigued me, because you don't seem to have that problem. So tell me this—how do you keep them from turning on you?"

Carlton gave a smug grin. "That's why Brenna is here."

Marcos's pulse picked up. This was exactly where he'd hoped Carlton would go with his answer. He feigned confusion. "Brenna? What does she have to do with anything? I mean, she said you two had business, but honestly, I figured it was minor. Doesn't she work for foster care? What can she offer you?" Carlton lifted an eyebrow, and Marcos let realization slowly show on his features. "You're using foster care kids? That's brilliant," he said, forcing admiration instead of disgust and anger into his voice. "But I thought Brenna grew up in the system? Now she's turning on it, handing over kids?"

How had his foster father gotten involved all those years ago? In retrospect, Marcos realized that the home office where the fire had started was a little strange for a factory worker to need—unless he was involved in some other business, too. But it was hardly a smoking gun. Had their foster father been an indirect connection—had he somehow gotten files on kids by pretending to be interested in helping them after they got out of the system? If so, maybe the system had started to get suspicious. Maybe Carlton hoped Brenna would be a more direct route.

"Not yet," Carlton said. "But the source we've always used is getting ready to retire." He laughed. "And she doesn't even know she's a source! And this time, I'm going to be in charge of the source directly. Brenna still needs testing, but I've dug into her. She's got an angry streak, and we just need to pull it out, use it to our advantage."

Marcos nodded slowly, pretending to consider, when inside he was marveling at how wrong Carlton had it. Brenna didn't have an angry streak; she had a compassionate streak. And that was going to be Carlton's undoing.

"Happy now?" Carlton asked, standing. "You got your question. And I got some answers. Now head to bed. We have an early morning."

"Wait," Marcos pressed. "I said the idea was brilliant, not that it was a guarantee. How can—"

"These kids have no one," Carlton said. "I fill that void, but of course, not directly. They can't identify me even if they wanted to, and they're not about to turn on the one person who's offered them help."

"None of them can identify you? You use a middleman?"

"Something like that," Carlton said.

The brief hesitation told Marcos *some* of those kids could identify him, which matched Brenna's story that she'd first identified Carlton leaving Simon Mellor's place.

"Besides," Carlton said, "what you got this morning was a second chance. You're one of the few. I don't offer those to dealers who screw up."

"You kill them?"

Carlton smiled. "I've never killed anyone."

Right, Marcos thought.

Carlton held out a hand, gesturing to the door. As Marcos was walking through it, Carlton reminded him, "Early tomorrow. You've got one last test, and then the real fun begins."

Marcos said goodnight and hurried to his room, feeling the same foreboding as when he'd first arrived. Did Carlton suspect something? He'd seemed satisfied enough to give Marcos details, and Marcos knew he hadn't misspoken on any of his backstory. But he didn't like the sound of Carlton's morning "test."

Stripping down to his boxer briefs, he yanked back the covers on his bed. And then he swore loudly enough that he worried for a moment he'd bring Carlton from across the house.

Because curled up under his covers was Brenna.

Chapter Eight

"Are you crazy?" Marcos demanded.

Brenna blinked up at him, too distracted by the wide, bare expanse of his chest to really comprehend his words. He wore nothing but a pair of snug boxer briefs, and even in the dim light of the one lamp lit in the room, she could see he took good care of himself. The man was covered in muscles that seemed to tense as her gaze shifted over them. Even the big bruise snaking up the right side of his stomach and the matching bruises on his arms didn't detract from how attractive he was.

"Brenna," Marcos snapped, grabbing his jeans off the floor and yanking them back on. Instead of buttoning them, he took her arm and pulled her out of his bed.

She hadn't intended to fall asleep. Really, she'd had no intention of going anywhere near Marcos's bed, with or without him in it. And from the way he was glaring at her now, he didn't want that, either.

She flushed, because with his obvious anger, she should have been less attracted to him. Instead, standing this close to him, she felt like she couldn't get enough air into her lungs.

And when she finally lifted her gaze to his eyes, she realized beneath the anger at her being in his room was something else. Something he was clearly trying to hide. Maybe it was the undercover training that made him so good at concealing his emotions, but even that didn't eliminate the desire in his eyes as he stared back at her.

A smile trembled on the corners of her lips.

"This isn't funny," he whispered. "If Carlton catches you in here, he's going to lose it. And I'm still healing from the first beating."

Any amusement instantly fled. Her free hand lifted, pressing flat against his abdomen, where that nasty purple bruise marred the perfection of his body.

He hissed in a breath.

"Did I hurt you?"

"No," he groaned, pulling her hand away. "Brenna, what are you doing in here?"

"Sorry." She stepped back, trying to regain her equilibrium, and bumped the bed. She swallowed, sidestepping it and crossing her arms over her chest. "Look, I—I messed up."

"Yeah, well, slip back to your room now, and it should be fine. Just don't get caught."

"It's too late."

"Someone saw you come in here?" he demanded.

"No. But while you were meeting with Carlton, I thought I'd take a peek in his bedroom."

Marcos sighed. "Why? What did you expect to find in there?"

"Something," Brenna replied, frustrated that he was angry with her for doing her job. "Anything. I can't take years of this, tiptoeing around Carlton's interest in me, pretending to leak him information so we can catch him. What happens in the meantime? I want to bring him down *now*."

"Yeah, I get that."

"I don't think you do. You got a family out of foster care. Even with the fire, even being split up, you and Cole and Andre found each other again. Me, I got ripped out of there and—"

Emotions overwhelmed her, the memory of standing in that hospital, watching them take Cole into a room beside her, his hands blistering and red, with Andre running after him. Begging the nurse to tell her where Marcos was, and hearing only that he was okay. Being shuttled into a car with some woman from Child and Family Services she'd never met. She'd watched out the window of that sedan until the hospital disappeared. She'd never seen any of them again. Not Marcos, Cole or Andre. Not the other two foster boys who'd lived at that house, or their foster parents, the Pikes. From that moment on, she'd really, truly been alone.

It had been nothing compared to the complete devastation of losing her mom a few months before that, of waking up in the wrecked car off the side of the road, bleeding and cold. Rescue workers telling her she'd be okay. But she'd seen her mom in the front seat, her head slumped sideways, no one helping her because it was already too late.

A few months later, she'd just started to come out of the numbness that had filled her. She'd just begun to feel like maybe one day she'd smile again. It had been Marcos who'd made her feel that way, and then he'd been ripped away, too.

"Brenna," Marcos whispered, his tone softer now, his hand palming her cheek.

She stepped quickly out of his reach, sucking in a calming breath, and spoke the other part of what had brought her here. "A kid died in my arms, Marcos. Eighteen. He was too far gone to even tell me his name." Sitting on the cold pavement, cradling his head in her lap as his blood soaked through her clothes, had taken her instantly back to those moments in the car with her mom, helpless to do anything.

She was going to lose it. *Don't cry*, Brenna pleaded with herself, shoving the memories into the back of her mind, where they were least likely to ambush her.

Marcos had stepped closer again, and Brenna held out her hand, flat-palmed against the center of his bare chest. "Don't. I'm fine. Look, I just—"

"This is personal," Marcos finished for her.

"Yes."

"For me, too," Marcos said, reaching up and taking the hand she was holding him away with and twining his fingers with hers. "You say this is connected to our past, and I want to know how. Because Carlton told me the reason he needs you is that his connection in foster care is retiring. That she doesn't even know she's his source."

"She," Brenna repeated.

"Yeah, *she*. Which means it can't be our foster father."

"That can't be right," Brenna insisted. "I know what I saw."

"It was a long time ago," Marcos reminded

her, still way too distracted by her nearness. She had such soft, tiny hands, and there'd been so much vulnerability in her eyes when she'd talked about her past. And yet, she was here, in the den of a sociopath drug lord, risking her life. She was way stronger than she looked.

"Yeah, well, that day is pretty stamped in my memory."

"Mine, too," Marcos replied. "But maybe the papers aren't what you thought they were." When she tried to interrupt, he said over her, "Or maybe they weren't his."

"You think they were our foster mother's? That he found them, and that's why he was looking at them late at night?"

"Maybe."

"But she didn't work for the foster system, either."

"No," Marcos agreed. "Not that we know of. But she did work out of the house, part-time. Maybe her work was somehow connected."

Brenna shook her head. "No, I double-checked all of that. I can't find any connection between either of them to the system. Not to their biological son, either—he owns his own business, nothing to do with foster care."

Marcos frowned at her. "Then why are you so convinced our foster father is connected? That was a long time ago, and Carlton's operation was just getting off the ground back then. And I have to tell you, the way Carlton talked about the whole thing, I'm not even sure he's the one who found the source. Sounds like it was someone else in his organization, and that this time, he's happy because you're going to be *his* in directly." The thought gave Marcos pause—the way Carlton had said it, it had sounded almost like there was someone else who had as much, or more, power than him and he wanted to steal it. But that didn't make any sense, and he shook it off as Brenna jumped in.

"I know what I saw back then," Brenna insisted. "And I don't know how our foster father is connected, but I know he is."

Marcos nodded slowly. Logically, it seemed like a stretch, but he could see how strongly Brenna believed it. Sometimes memories could betray you—gaining conviction over time, twisting and becoming unreliable. But he'd been an agent for a long time, and he also knew the power of a cop's gut. "Okay, I believe you."

She seemed surprised. "You do?"

"Yeah." He grinned at her, less stressed now that the initial surprise of finding her in his bed had worn off, and more intrigued. He was still holding her hand, and he turned it palm up and stroked the sensitive skin with his fingers.

"Now, why don't you tell me what you were doing in my bed?"

Her fingers twitched, then curled inward. Her gaze dipped, lingering on his bare chest before meeting his again. "Uh—"

He took a step closer, suddenly uncaring that they were in Carlton's house. The drug lord had gone to bed. The guards he had left—hopefully—had gone to bed, too. No one had to know Brenna wasn't in her own room.

And it didn't matter how many years had passed, how much he still didn't know about her. He recalled the power of that first crush eighteen years ago. It had been sudden, like a sucker punch to the gut, only instead of leaving him in pain, it had made the world seem wonderful. Seeing her again, even under these circumstances, and he had that very same feeling.

"Marcos," she whispered, her eyes dilating as she tipped her head back.

He kept hold of her hand, sliding his other one around her waist and pulling her close. She gasped at the full-body contact, and he swallowed it, pressing his lips to hers as her free hand wound around his neck.

She fit. The words rattled in his desire-fogged brain, and he knew it was more than the way her body molded so perfectly to his.

Eighteen years should have been more than

enough time to move on. They'd both changed so much since those brief months they'd spent together, just trying to understand their place in the world, to find a real connection. Somehow, they'd both ended up in law enforcement, and when she'd said she didn't have a boyfriend, he'd known instantly that it was the same reason he'd never stuck around in a serious relationship. If he was being honest with himself, it was fear. Fear of a real connection that would disappear the way everything seemed to in his childhood.

But he wasn't a child anymore, and neither was she. He tilted his head, trying to get better access as her mouth glided over his again and again. The instant he slipped his tongue past the seam of her lips, she moaned and arched up, freeing their linked hands and grasping his back for better leverage.

He reached for her hand, hoping to redirect it around his neck, but it was too late. She froze and pulled her head away, her eyes wide.

"Marcos," she whispered, stepping out of his embrace and trying to turn him.

He planted his feet and refused to let himself be moved. "It was a long time ago."

Tears welled up in her eyes and one of them slipped free, running down her cheek and getting caught in the Cupid's bow above her mouth.

He reached out and swiped it free, taking her hands in his and trying to pull them up around his neck. "Come here."

She resisted. "Show me."

"It's not pretty," he warned her, nervous even though he knew physical scars wouldn't scare her off. People had seen the scars before, and he'd given the quick, easy truth: "Burns from a fire, a long time ago."

But it was different when he was showing someone who had been in that fire with him. Someone who—whether she admitted it or not—already felt guilty about the way the fire had started.

This time, he let her turn him slowly. She gasped when she saw his back, but he'd expected as much. What he didn't expect was to feel her fingertips glide over the mass of scar tissue that covered his back and then her lips to follow.

He drew in a breath. The pajama pants he'd worn to bed the night of the fire had been cotton—they'd caught fire, but not badly. But his top had been synthetic. The fire had sucked that material right into his skin.

The doctors had done their best, and the scars on other parts of his body—the ones the fire had left on the backs of his legs, the ones the glass had left on his face and hands when

he'd dived through the window to escape—
were almost entirely gone now. But his back?

He recalled the moment he'd tripped on those
stairs, running down from the bedroom he'd
shared with Cole and Andre. One minute they'd
been in front of him. When he'd pushed back
to his feet, they'd been gone, through a doorway he couldn't follow because flames leaped
in their place. He'd gone the other way, the fire
chasing him, and done the only thing he could
do as it finally caught up to him: dived through
the living room window.

When he'd landed on the grass in front of the
house, he'd thought he was dying. He'd sensed
Andre talking to him through his own tears,
felt the weight of Cole's hands as they patted
out the fire. Then he'd been loaded into an ambulance and passed out.

He'd woken in the hospital, a pain more intense than he'd ever known that seemed to heat
every part of his body. But it was centered on
his back. After a few months, he'd actually felt
less on his back, from the nerve damage. But
right now, despite how thick the scar tissue
was, each light touch of Brenna's lips made his
nerves wake up, sent desire spiraling through
his body.

Marcos closed his eyes and let himself feel,
then spun back around and captured her lips

with his again. They tasted salty now, and he realized she'd been crying.

Instead of the frantic kisses from earlier, this time was slower, sweeter. When her arms went back around him, settling around his waist, it didn't bother him. In fact, it felt right. He pressed his mouth to hers, ready to stay there for a long, long time, when she pulled free.

"Marcos, I need to tell you something."

His fingers slipped under the hem of her T-shirt, discovering the skin there was somehow even softer than her palm. "Mmm. Can you tell me later?"

"No." She slipped out of his arms, stepping back and bumping the bed. Her voice was throaty, her lips swollen from his kisses. "Marcos, I just got tired waiting for you. I didn't mean to fall asleep. I didn't intend for you to find me in your bed."

"Okay," he replied slowly. Was she trying to tell him she didn't want to jump into bed? "That's all right. We don't have to rush into anything." He moved toward her. "I just want to kiss you for a few hours."

She let out a noise that could have been anticipation, could have been surprise. But she put her hand up on his chest again. "No, I mean, I was waiting here to tell you something."

"Okay." He took her hand the way he had

before, smiling at her, hoping it would work a second time as he drew circles on her palm. He was about to lower his head and trace them with his tongue when her words stopped him.

"Carlton's nephew caught me in the office."

Chapter Nine

"What happened?" Marcos demanded.

Brenna tried to focus, but her lips still tingled from his mouth and her fingertips still felt the uneven surface of his back. If only she hadn't gone downstairs for a drink of water in the middle of the night all those years ago. Things might have been so different.

Marcos wouldn't have the scars. It made her want to cry all over again, thinking of the pain he must have gone through. Maybe, if the fire had never happened, they all would have stayed together.

What had Marcos looked like as a teenager? What had he done when he hit eighteen and been kicked out of the system? What had made him decide to go into law enforcement? She wished she'd been there for all of those things.

But she couldn't go back and change any of it. All she could hope to do was make some kind of restitution now, by ensuring whatever her foster father had been doing that night ended.

"Brenna," Marcos prompted, and she forced her mind back on the present. "I thought you said you looked in Carlton's bedroom?"

"I thought that's what it was. But he has a second office." She could see Marcos's instant interest and she nodded. "Lots of desk drawers and file cabinets, but they were all locked. I didn't have time to pick them. I'm not sure I got anything useful." She was about to tell him about the paper she'd grabbed when he spoke.

"What did you tell Jesse?"

"I said I got confused, that the house is like a maze. I wasn't in there very long, and I know he wasn't following me. He looked really surprised to see me when he flipped the light on."

"Well, that's believable. The house *is* like a maze, I think on purpose. But what was *Jesse* doing in there? Carlton doesn't seem like the type of guy who'd let people hang out in his personal office."

"I don't know." After her immediate relief that it wasn't Carlton, she'd wondered the same thing. "He didn't say."

"Did he buy your explanation?"

"I think so. I asked him not to tell Carlton—played it like I was nervous about what happened earlier, that it was an accident, but I didn't want him mad at me. Jesse seemed to understand that concept really well. Honestly, I got the impression he didn't want Carlton to know he'd been in there, either."

"So, you think you're safe? Or do we need to run now?"

She gaped at him. "We?" She shook her head. "Even if I'm compromised, you didn't vouch for me. Whatever happens to me, I won't betray your cover. This is about me."

"No, it's not." She realized he'd never let go of her hand as his fingers tightened around hers. "We're a team now, you and me."

The idea flooded her with warmth, made her feel more secure and more afraid at the same time. She'd never let herself lean on someone, and the idea of leaning on Marcos now was way too tempting, for too many reasons. But the opposite was also true. If she didn't rely on anyone but herself and messed up, then no one else would get hurt.

If this were just about her, she wouldn't have hesitated. It was worth the risk.

But it was no longer just about her. "I don't think he's going to say anything, but I can't be positive."

Marcos nodded, stepping a little closer. "Noth-

ing in life is a guarantee, especially in undercover work."

Her pulse picked up again at his nearness,
her body wanting to lean into him. She stiffened, trying to let her mind rule. "What do you
think we should do?"

"If you don't think you're compromised, we
stay."

If she stayed here much longer, she was definitely going to be compromised, but in a completely different way.

As if Marcos could read her thoughts, a little
smile tipped the corners of his lips, and then he
was lowering his head to hers again. He tasted
like the Bordeaux they'd drunk with dinner, in-
toxicating and rich. He tasted like every dream
she'd had as an eleven-year-old girl, discovering her very first taste of love.

Love. The idea had her stumbling backward.

"What's wrong?" Marcos asked.

The concern on his face made her want to
touch him even more. She folded her hands
behind her back. "I should go." She sounded
breathy and nervous, and silently she cursed
herself. "I want to get back to my room before
Carlton's other bodyguards start their nightly
rounds."

"They have nightly rounds?" Marcos asked,

but he seemed way more interested in letting his eyes roam over her than the answer.

"Yes." Or if they didn't, someone had a serious sleepwalking problem, because she'd heard footsteps pass her room regularly last night. She glanced down at her watch, realizing that she really did need to slip back to her room soon.

On impulse, she leaned forward and pressed a brief, last kiss to his lips, then ran to the door. Peeking through it, her heart thundered in her chest, but not because she was afraid of getting caught so much as she was afraid to stay.

Puppy love was completely different from real love, she reminded herself. And that's what she had with Marcos—a lingering infatuation she'd never really been able to get out of her system. It was made worse because he'd been the thing that kept her going all those years in foster care. The idea of one day emerging on the other side of the system, to find him waiting for her.

But that's all it had been—a perfect, impossible idea. That's all Marcos was right now, too. She didn't really know the man, just the pedestal she'd put him on all her life.

She glanced back at him one last time, then darted into the empty hallway. All the way back to her room, she wondered if going undercover in the lair of a crazy drug lord wasn't the most dangerous thing she'd done this weekend. It was being in close proximity to Marcos that could really be her undoing.

"WE HAVE A traitor in our midst," Carlton announced calmly at breakfast.

Marcos paused, a bite of Parisian omelet halfway to his mouth. He let his gaze move slowly over to Carlton, not to dart around the room and linger on Brenna the way instinct would have him do. Which one of them had Carlton discovered? Marcos prayed it was him.

All last night, after Brenna had left his room, he'd tossed and turned, unable to sleep. He couldn't keep his mind from wandering to the sweetness of her mouth, the softness of her skin under his hands. He couldn't keep from thinking about what an amazing woman she'd become, from wondering about all the years in between now and when he'd last seen her.

"What are you talking about?" Brenna asked when the silence dragged out.

She sounded nervous, a little defiant, but those should have been believable reactions even if she was completely innocent. Because the reality was, *completely innocent* was a stretch for the person she was pretending to be.

"Why don't you tell her, Marco?" Carlton asked, his cold blue gaze locking on Marcos.

He should have felt terrified. Out in the Appalachians without a weapon and surrounded by Carlton and all the guards he had left—which, from what Marcos could tell, were the two regular guards standing against the wall, plus the knife-wielding chef in the kitchen, and Jesse.

Instead, he was relieved. As long as Brenna's cover wasn't blown, maybe he could talk his way out of this. It wouldn't be the first time a drug lord had suspected he was in law enforcement. Actually, any drug lord with any sense at all would suspect everyone he did business with could be an undercover agent. Besides, Carlton hadn't used Marcos's real name, which meant whatever he thought he knew, he didn't have the full truth.

Marcos calmly set down his fork. He didn't have to look around the table to sense the tension increase. Jesse was a ball of nerves at all times, and Brenna was new to undercover. She wouldn't be used to this kind of constant testing.

Marcos prayed that's all it was, that Carlton hadn't discovered his real identity. But Carlton had promised him one last test this morning, and Marcos hoped this was it.

"I'm not sure I can," Marcos replied.

Carlton smiled, but there was nothing happy about it. He looked like a snake ready to pounce. "No?"

His attention shifted to Brenna, across the table from Marcos. "How about you?"

Marcos let his gaze shift to her, watched her narrowing eyes as she folded her arms across her chest. She was dressed in jeans and a long-sleeved red shirt today, and it looked so much more natural on her than the skintight dresses. Although he couldn't say he minded the dresses, this felt like the real Brenna. And the real Brenna was a lot harder to resist than the person she was pretending to be.

"This isn't what I signed up for," Brenna said, her tone a mix of fear and defiance. "This was supposed to be simple business, not beatings and accusations and..." Her voice trailed off, then she finished, "I had to shoot someone, Carlton, and whether it was your intention or not, I felt like I didn't have a choice. I'm looking for security. I'm not some kind of crazy adrenaline junkie."

"Don't forget that was my man you shot," Carlton said.

She set her napkin over her half-eaten omelet and stood. "I don't think I'm cut out for this."

"Sit down," Carlton snapped.

When she didn't immediately comply, one of his guards stepped forward from the corner and put his hands on her shoulders, shoving her back down.

Marcos felt his entire body tense, wanting to lay the man out for touching her, but he tried to keep the fury off his face. If this *was* a test, Brenna was playing it exactly right.

She glared up at the guard but kept quiet.

"It's too late to back out now, my dear. You're going to be *my* ticket," Carlton told her.

Marcos frowned, wondering once again if Carlton had someone else in the organization they didn't know about, perhaps a second in command who ran the current foster care connection. Maybe Carlton wanted to handle it himself. It would mean more possibilities for leaks to law enforcement, but also more power.

"And anyway, you're not the one I'm worried about," Carlton said. "I've got security cameras at my front door. I've got your little shooting on tape. Some creative editing, darling, and unless you want to try to explain murder to the police, I *own* you."

She stiffened, her fingers curling around the tabletop until they turned white, but she still didn't say a word.

This time, Carlton's smile was more genuine. "Don't worry. You'll still have your *security*. I just like some extra insurance, and your little display yesterday made it simple. It wasn't exactly what I had planned, but—" he shrugged "—you showed me I need to be more careful who I hire to keep me safe."

The guards behind Brenna stood straighter, their muscles tensing at the implication they might be on the chopping block, too.

"So, you think *I'm* a traitor?" Marcos spoke up, wanting to get Carlton's attention off Brenna. "Why, exactly? Because all I've done is try to talk about getting some of your product to my networks. Is this your idea of one last test? Call me a traitor and see if I lose it? My family has done worse than that."

Carlton sneered. "Your family can't protect you here. And I see I haven't underestimated your intelligence, Marco. This *is* one last test. Because I'm not accusing you, either."

"Then who, exactly?" Marcos asked, but he suddenly dreaded the answer, because he knew what Carlton was going to say before he spoke.

Carlton's gaze moved to the last person seated at the table. "I never thought I'd have to eliminate yet another person of my own flesh and blood."

Jesse stood, shaking his head. His face flushed a deep, angry red—but from fear or anger, Marcos wasn't sure.

What did Carlton mean by *another* person? The DEA knew Carlton was a killer, but they had no intel on the man taking out anyone in his own family.

Marcos glanced from Carlton back to Jesse and realization made the omelet flip in his stomach. The car accident that had killed Jesse's parents and left the kid in Carlton's care. It had been deemed an accident. Lots of snow, slippery roads, combined with a blown tire had been fatal. But maybe that blown tire hadn't been an accident. What had Jesse discovered?

He held in a string of curses as Jesse insisted, "Uncle Carlton, I swear, I didn't betray you. Please—"

"You think I don't know you've been in my office?" Carlton boomed.

Both Jesse and Brenna jerked, and Marcos hoped Carlton hadn't also realized Brenna had been in his office.

"I doubt—" Marcos started.

"Did I ask your opinion?" Carlton yelled.

"Uncle—" Jesse begged.

"Stop! You can't explain this away," Carlton said, suddenly calm.

"He brought me here to you, to do business," Marcos said. "Why would he do that if he was betraying you?" He knew he was stepping into dangerous territory, opening the door to the idea that he was also a traitor, but Marcos couldn't stand by and watch Carlton kill his nephew.

Carlton's shrewd gaze shifted to Marcos, and he pressed his luck. "He's practically still a kid. There's no need to hurt him."

"Oh, I'm not going to hurt him," Carlton replied evenly. "This is your test. You're going to do it for me."

Chapter Ten

"I'm not the only one who was in—" Jesse started.

Marcos cut him off fast, before he finished that sentence and told his uncle that Brenna had also been in his office. "This is crazy," Marcos said. "Just because the kid was in your office isn't a sign of betrayal. I did the same thing to my dad—I wanted to know more about his business than he was willing to tell me."

The "kid" was twenty-four—only six years younger than Marcos. But for some reason, every time Marcos looked at him, he saw a scared boy pretending to be a badass.

Carlton's eyes narrowed on him, and Marcos couldn't tell if he was pissing the drug lord off or getting through to him, so he rushed on. "It wasn't betrayal for me, either. I just wanted to be part of it. I wanted to be like him."

Marcos nodded at Jesse and watched Carlton's gaze follow.

Jesse was sweating, his entire body shaking. He had a deer-in-the-headlights look, but at least the fear was keeping him quiet, giving Marcos a chance to talk.

"Your nephew and I met up and played pool about a million times before I got the invite up here," Marcos continued. "And all he did was brag about you. No details, of course, but he didn't need to do that. I already knew who you were. Just hero worship."

It wasn't exactly true, but it was close. Jesse adored the uncle who had taken him in after his parents died. But the adoration had felt a little forced, as though Jesse knew he shouldn't put his lot in with a criminal.

"Is that right?" Carlton asked, crossing his beefy arms over his chest and leaning back in his chair.

Was he pushing too much? Marcos wondered. Was Carlton about to turn on both of them? Only one way to know for sure.

"Yes. And look, I know you wanted me to vouch for Brenna here." He glanced at her, shrugged in feigned apology. "But I couldn't— don't know her well enough. But your nephew? I'd vouch for him. No way would he turn on you."

"That seems awfully foolish," Carlton said, as Jesse glanced between them hopefully. "For all you know, I have absolute proof of his betrayal and you've just signed your own death warrant alongside him."

Jesse went so pale Marcos thought he was going to pass out. One of the guards must have expected Jesse to run, because the guard stepped in front of the doorway, blocking the exit.

"I don't think you do," Marcos said, keeping his tone casual, almost cocky.

"No? And why exactly would the son of an organized crime boss vouch for an orphan?"

Jesse jerked, then pulled himself straighter, like he'd been insulted by his uncle's categorization of him, then gotten defiant. But thank goodness, he was keeping his mouth shut about one thing he'd seen in his uncle's office: Brenna.

Marcos shrugged. "I don't know how you get your kicks, but I don't kill kids. If you're looking for leverage on me, you'll have to find it some other way."

Carlton's expression got so dark so fast that Marcos knew he'd just pushed the drug lord too far.

"I don't think so," Carlton said, standing and snapping his fingers.

His guards' weapons came out, pointed at Marcos.

Carlton reached behind his back and revealed his own pistol. He emptied all the bullets on the table, except the one in the chamber, then handed it to Marcos. "Either you kill him, or they kill you."

BRENNA'S HAND CURLED around the butter knife she'd palmed almost as soon as she'd sat down for breakfast. It was instinct—had been for years, ever since that third foster home. She couldn't help herself.

The urge had faded as she'd gotten older. Instead of stealing dull knives everywhere she went, she'd started carrying a tactical knife on her at all times. Then, she'd joined the police force, and when she was on duty, she had her service pistol.

But up here in the mountains, with Carlton Wayne White, unarmed for her cover, she'd fallen right back into her old habits. She had a collection of Carlton's butter knives in her room. She was sure he—or his chef—had noticed by now, but no one had said anything. They probably figured it was irrelevant, that she either had a theft problem or that it wasn't going to make much difference against a pack of guns.

They were right about that. But as her gaze swiveled from Carlton, smirking from the head of the table, to Marcos, way calmer than he should have been, to Jesse, terrified in the corner as one of Carlton's guards disarmed him, her grip tightened. She'd never live through attacking a pair of guards with a butter knife. And even if she did, she knew for a fact that Carlton was concealing more than just the gun he'd handed to Marcos.

Her heartbeat pounded in her ears as she prepared herself for a last stand. After all these years, she'd finally found Marcos Costa, only to die with him. She blinked back tears, wishing she'd stayed with him last night. Wishing she had at least that memory now.

"This is crazy," she said, needing to give reason one last try. "Why does anyone have to die? I thought this was a professional business operation." Her voice came out too high-pitched and panicky, and she didn't even need to force it.

"You want to play in the big leagues, you'd better get used to it," Carlton told her.

Ever since she'd turned down sleeping with him, he'd been far less interested in keeping her happy. Carlton's temper—and his unpredictability—were legendary. She'd known that before she'd pressed her boss to let her come up here. But she'd never seen him like this. It almost made her wonder if he was using his own product.

But no, the truth was much scarier. The truth was that he was really willing to watch his own nephew—and anyone else in his way—die to protect his business.

She stared at Marcos, praying that his years at the DEA, which involved a lot of undercover work, had given him practice in situations like this. That maybe he had a way out.

But he seemed as shocked as she felt. He glanced down at the pistol in his hand, then back up at Carlton. The cocky, drug-dealer expression he wore around Carlton was gone, replaced by a seriousness she'd only seen when they were alone.

"Uncle Carlton," Jesse pleaded, his voice barely more than a whisper. "I was just looking for—"

"I know what you were looking for," Carlton replied. "And I'm sorry, kid. I really was hoping to groom you to work with me at a higher level." He shrugged. "But if I can't trust you, there's no way I can let you disrupt everything I've worked for all these years."

Jesse glanced at Marcos, then at her, like he was hoping one of them would come to his rescue, but all Brenna could do was stare back at him, helpless.

His gaze swung quickly back to his uncle, and Brenna thought he was going to blurt out that he'd seen her in Carlton's office, too. Instead, he asked softly, "Did you really kill my parents?"

"Nah, I didn't kill them," Carlton said, but there was nothing truthful in his voice.

He turned to Marcos. "Let's do this outside. I don't need a mess in here."

Carlton nodded at a guard, who grabbed Jesse and forced him to the door. He nodded for Marcos to follow, and when Brenna didn't move, he told her, "Let's go."

"I'm not watching this." Her feet felt glued to the floor. She couldn't just watch Jesse die, no matter what he did for a living. But how could she prevent it? If she went after a guard again, she'd be shot by the second one or by Carlton. This time, no one was going to underestimate her.

"Yes, you are," Carlton said, gripping the top of her arm so hard she knew it would leave a bruise.

She kept the knife flat against the inside of her arm, letting him drag her outside, because the truth was, she couldn't hide from this, either. Panic set in as they all stepped into the wilderness surrounding Carlton's home.

No one would hear the shot. And Marcos would become a killer.

"I HAVE A better idea," Marcos announced, taking in the gorgeous wilderness that surrounded Carlton's home.

The trees were really changing color now, fiery reds and oranges, with greens mixed in from the fir trees. He could hear birds in the distance, and the crisp air seemed to clear his mind.

"I'm getting tired of your stalling," Carlton said. He had a tight grip on Brenna, keeping her close, as though she might run and take out another of his guards.

The two guards had positioned themselves on opposite sides of Marcos, and the one who'd been holding on to Jesse shoved him, sending him sprawling to the ground.

Jesse skidded through a pile of dead leaves, but didn't bother trying to get up. He was crying now, silent sobs that sent tears and snot running down his face. But he'd stopped begging, probably knowing his uncle too well.

"Hear me out," Marcos insisted, the plan forming in his head as he spoke. It was a long shot, but he'd spent months reading up on everything the DEA knew about Carlton Wayne White before he'd even approached Jesse.

No one could identify how exactly Carlton had gotten started, but he was a perfect fit as a drug lord. Not only did he look the part—like someone no one would want to mess with—but even before he hit the DEA's radar, he'd had a reputation. As a kid, he'd been to juvie a few times, but he'd learned fast how to hide what he was doing.

In his early twenties, he'd become a boxer, and he'd been the guy who went for the KO right away and then immediately wanted a new opponent. His trainers had spent a long time convincing him to draw out the fight, to make it a show. But when he'd finally agreed to do it, he'd clearly gotten joy out of taunting the poor sucker scheduled to fight him.

Marcos knew Carlton liked the lead-up as much as the knockout, maybe even more so. "Even though I still think this is unnecessary, what's the fun of shooting someone in the head?"

Carlton smirked. "If you have to ask, you're not doing it right."

Beside him, Brenna was unnaturally still, her arm up at a weird angle as Carlton kept a grip on it. But that wasn't entirely why, Marcos realized. She was holding her arm awkwardly because she was hiding something.

No way had she gotten a gun into Carlton's

mansion without it being taken away from her immediately, so what? He tried to figure it out, but gave up after a few seconds. He had more important things to worry about right now.

Jesse had picked himself off the ground, wiped his face on his sleeve and was now standing defiantly, his chin up as he stared at his uncle.

"Come on," Marcos said, moving in a slow circle, gesturing to the nature around them. "You have all *this* and you want to use a gun?"

Carlton's eyes narrowed. He was either intrigued or starting to get suspicious about why Marcos wasn't pulling the trigger.

Marcos spoke quickly. "Let me work him over, then send him off. No one's going to help him, right? Not if he shows up with a shiner. They'd never mess with you by taking him in. And it took me forever to get up here, find this place. He's not making it back to civilization. It'll be starvation or hypothermia or some animal attracted to the blood."

Brenna's mouth dropped open, and she shook her head, like she couldn't believe what he was saying.

He avoided her gaze, not wanting her to think less of him. If Carlton went for his plan, it wouldn't be pretty. But at least it would keep the kid alive for the immediate future, give him a chance, unlike a bullet to the head—inevitable even if Marcos refused. Then it would be up to Jesse.

Carlton's gaze dropped to Brenna, then back up to Marcos, a slow smile spreading. "You're a lot crueler than I'd figured, Marco."

He shrugged, hoping he looked blasé with his heart racing, a pistol with one bullet clutched in a death grip in his hand. "Yeah, well, I come by it naturally. You know who my family is." It was a subtle reminder not to push him too far.

The drug lord nodded slowly, and Marcos held his breath, hoping he'd agree. It wasn't an ideal solution, but it was better than a shoot-out with one bullet on his side and whatever Brenna had clutched in her hand.

"Okay," Carlton agreed, and Marcos let out the breath he'd been holding. "Do it, but hand over that gun first."

Hoping Carlton hadn't just decided to shoot *him* in the head instead, Marcos held out the pistol.

Carlton had to step forward to grab it, and he let go of Brenna's arm. She tucked that arm close to her, confirming Marcos's suspicion that she had some kind of weapon.

"Now do it," Carlton said, holding the gun on him.

Marcos turned toward Jesse, who'd stiffened his spine and his jaw. He wanted to mouth an apology to the kid, but although Carlton was at his back, the guards would see it.

So, instead he pulled back his fist and swung. It landed with a solid crack, and Jesse flew backward into one of the guards.

The guard shoved him away, and Jesse fell face-first onto the ground as Brenna gasped.

It couldn't have gone better if Marcos had planned it that way. He got down next to Jesse, yanking him back to his feet with one hand, and slipping his car keys into the kid's hoodie pocket with the other. Then, he hit the kid again, pain knotting his stomach as if he were taking the punch instead of giving it.

Jesse went down again without a fight, just another grunt of pain. This time, he pushed himself to his feet, blood dripping from one corner of his mouth.

"Again," Carlton ordered.

"Carlton," Brenna protested.

"Again!"

"Stop!" Brenna yelled.

Marcos swung again. He tried to aim for places that would split skin and cause bleeding, but wouldn't do too much other damage, but he had to be careful. Carlton had been a boxer—he knew his punches.

This time, when Jesse went down, he pushed himself to his knees, then flopped to the ground again. He tried to get up again and stumbled into Marcos, who shoved him away, making sure to push the keys into the kid's stomach through his hoodie.

Please get the message, Marcos willed. Carlton's guards had moved Marcos's car into an outbuilding, then returned the keys to him with a warning not to go anywhere without Carlton's say-so. It was far enough away that Jesse could circle back and take it, hopefully after dark when there was less of a chance of one of Carlton's guards spotting him.

Once the car made it to civilization and Marcos didn't check in, a pack of DEA agents would surround it, since the phone tucked into the car's hidey-hole was tagged with a GPS tracker. When they found Jesse inside instead of him, they'd protect him. They'd also send a bunch of armed agents to retrieve Marcos.

Which meant time was running out if he wanted to gather evidence on Carlton. This was about to be the end of his undercover operation.

"Now, go," Carlton told his nephew.

Jesse gave his uncle one last lingering glance, full of betrayal and pain and hatred, then turned and walked into the wilderness.

Chapter Eleven

"Congratulations," Carlton told Marcos. "You passed my last test. You're in."

Marcos grinned as he walked by Brenna and headed back toward the house, but she could see the discomfort in his eyes, what it had cost him to beat up Jesse and send him to his death.

Bile gathered in Brenna's throat. Was this what it took to succeed undercover? In order to take down men like Carlton Wayne White, you had to become like them?

She couldn't do it.

How many times had Marcos faced similar situations undercover? How many decisions just like this one had he made over the years? And what had it done to him, having to make the choice between saving himself and saving a kid? Because it didn't matter that Jesse certainly belonged in jail himself for the things he'd done under his uncle's orders. At the end of the day, he was still young enough, probably hadn't yet crossed a line he couldn't come back from, that he had a chance to turn his life around. Or he might have, if he hadn't been sent out into the Appalachians to die.

"Brenna," Carlton snapped, bringing her attention back to him.

He was smirking at her, clearly amused by her reaction. But he didn't seem surprised; after all, she was pretending to be a foster care worker. She might have been willing to make a deal with the devil in exchange for her own security, but a woman like that still wouldn't be immune to violence.

Taking a deep breath of the bitterly cold air, Brenna tried to calm her racing heart. She couldn't stop herself from glancing back in the direction Jesse had gone, deeper into the mountains instead of toward civilization. Not that it would have mattered. It was a several-hour drive just to get out of the mountains, and even then, there was nothing around for miles, unless you could hot-wire a car someone had left before taking a wilderness hike.

And the threats were everywhere. Hypothermia was probably the biggest one, but the threat of other humans might not be far behind. Up here, people didn't ask questions first; trespassers were simply shot.

Marcos had been right when he'd listed Jesse's chances; the kid would never make it.

The desire to run after him, to try to help him, rose up hard, but Carlton was staring at her, one eyebrow raised and that pistol still clutched in his hand. She had no doubt he'd use it on her if she tried. And what could she really do, with no way to communicate with her fellow officers and no supplies other than a butter knife?

Failure and pain mixed together, reminding her of the day she'd knelt on the cold ground next to Simon Mellor and rested the kid's head in her lap. She'd ignored protocol and tried to stem his bleeding with her bare hands, even though she knew it was too late to save him.

With one last glance into the wilderness, Brenna walked back toward the house. Before she made it, Carlton grabbed her arm again.

Instinctively, she tried to jerk away, but his size wasn't for show. The guy was incredibly strong.

"I've been pretty understanding about your eccentricities, but that's an expensive set of flatware and I'm running out of knives."

She flushed and flipped her hand over, revealing the knife tucked against her arm. "It's—"

"Self-preservation," he finished for her. "Believe me, I understand the concept." He stared at her a minute longer, and she wasn't sure what he saw—probably fear and sadness and self-disgust—and then he told her, "Never mind. You keep it if it makes you feel better."

Then, he actually patted her on the back with his enormous paw, and she saw a flash of matching sadness in his eyes. Some part of him hadn't wanted to kill Jesse, she realized. But that brief hint of humanity didn't matter.

She nodded her thanks and turned away from him, striding into his house before he saw any other emotion on her face. Because her determination to bring him down had just doubled. And now she needed to do it fast, find a way to get out of here and get help before Jesse died in the Appalachian Mountains all alone.

"I DIDN'T MAKE the decision about Jesse lightly," Carlton told them, settling into the big chair in his living room and draping his arms over the edges. "But I want you to understand what happens to traitors. You're committed now, so I expect one hundred percent loyalty from here on out."

Marcos nodded solemnly as he sat across from Carlton, then glanced at Brenna. She stood frozen in the doorway. The expression on her face was unreadable, but her eyes were blazing with anger, fear and determination. He prayed that Carlton misunderstood which emotion was winning.

Her gaze met his only briefly before she ducked her head and took the remaining chair. She didn't have to say a word for him to know what had happened in those moments outside the house: she'd lost all respect for him.

The idea hurt more than it should have, and he wanted to explain his reasoning, but all he could do was continue his ruse with Carlton. At least it was working, because if Jesse was smart—if he waited until the cover of darkness and then took Marcos's car and booked it for civilization, then Marcos had until evening to make this happen.

The plan had always been to head home tonight. Although he'd hoped to be able to wrap up the weekend with enough for an arrest that would send Carlton away for the rest of his life, the truth was, it was unlikely. A smart drug lord would start out with a small transaction, give him just enough product to prove himself before moving to a bigger shipment. And Marcos needed serious quantity to put Carlton away for good.

He had no real hope of sticking with that plan now. Even if the DEA didn't swarm after Jesse showed up, if the kid had gotten the message, then Marcos had no vehicle. And while he was sure Brenna would give him a ride, it wasn't likely to go unnoticed that his car was missing from Carlton's outbuilding. If he left too early, it would be Carlton and his guards searching for Jesse instead of the DEA.

So, he needed to time this exactly right. Set up a deal with Carlton and get out of there in time to stop the DEA from blowing his cover, but still give Jesse a chance to escape.

He settled into his chair and crossed his legs at the ankles. He pasted a semi-bored expression on his face, as if beating up people and sending them to certain death was well within his comfort zone. Inside, though, he felt physically ill.

"What now?" Brenna asked, speaking up before he could.

Carlton smiled. "Now we make your boy toy over here happy. We talk business."

"Boy toy?" Marcos replied, trying to stay in character, trying not to imagine Jesse's eyes as he'd taken that final hit. Resolute to his fate, but determined to go out standing. "Sounds fun, but I'm no one's toy."

"We'll see," Carlton said.

Marcos could guess what he was thinking. To Carlton, Marcos was nothing but a chess piece on a much bigger board. Little did Carlton know, Marcos felt the same way about him.

Some of his colleagues at the DEA had questioned the intelligence of an operation that sent him alone into the home of a man as unpredictable as Carlton Wayne White. Carlton was flat-out crazy. If the DEA came in to rescue him and things went south, Marcos didn't doubt he'd go out in a blaze of glory if it meant taking out cops with him.

Marcos needed something substantial, and soon. He didn't want to risk having to bring Carlton in without enough. Flipping him to get to his suppliers wasn't an option as far as Marcos was concerned. If Carlton was making money on the backs of foster kids, then Marcos wanted him to rot in prison for the rest of his life now more than ever. Not making a deal with the DEA and skating by in a cushy minimum-security federal penitentiary.

So, right now, Marcos let the insult go and leaned forward. "All right, Carlton. Let's get down to it. I passed your test, and I know why we did it in front of your house. It had nothing to do with bloodying up your marble floors."

Carlton grinned and shrugged. "Hope you smiled for the cameras."

"You've got your leverage and that's fine," Marcos said. "It wouldn't exactly be the first time—my family plays similar games. Now let's skip over some BS small-level deal. You've got this area locked up, but I can move you into New York, get you hooked up with my existing networks. We work together and in a few years, we'll both be tripling our income."

Carlton grinned, and Marcos could practically see the dollar signs flashing in his eyes. Carlton glanced over at Brenna. "What do you think, my dear? You ready for the big leagues?"

Brenna's eyes sparked at the endearment, and Marcos was pretty sure that was why the drug lord did it. He knew it pissed her off, and he liked seeing just how far he could push people.

"I set you up, and you do the same for me," she said flatly. But there was a dark undercurrent to her voice that made Marcos nervous.

What she'd seen with Jesse had tapped into that compassionate streak she had, and he knew it had just made her drive to bring the drug lord down even stronger. But she didn't know his plan, couldn't know they needed to stretch out the timeline.

Even before she spoke, he knew she was going to go the other way—try to rush Carlton into a deal and get out of there, and go looking for help for Jesse. And that would destroy any chance Marcos had of getting Jesse to safety while still keeping his cover intact with Carlton.

"What do you say you work out the smaller details with Brenna later?" Marcos jumped in. "To start, I'm looking for twenty-five kilograms. I'll bring the cash at the same time, but we do the trade on neutral territory."

"What?" Carlton mocked, not even blinking at the size of the deal. "You afraid I'll rip you off?"

"Nah," Marcos replied, refusing to be baited. "If you're smart—and I know you are—you're looking for a long-term relationship, not a one-off deal. But that doesn't mean I'm letting your goons take a piece of me again."

Carlton's guards tensed from where they'd taken up position near the doorway, and Carlton scowled.

"Glad you reminded me of that, Marco. Because you're going to add the cost of two new *goons* to the price of the shipment." Carlton glanced from him to Brenna. "Unless you think Brenna here should split the cost with you."

Not liking the implication Carlton put behind the word *cost*, Marcos shook his head. "It's fine. What's another fifty grand? But we do that, and the initial shipment goes up, too. Thirty kilos."

Carlton smiled slowly. "You really live up

to the Costrales name, Marco." He leaned forward, held out a beefy hand. When Marcos took it, he said, "You've got yourself a deal."

BRENNA TOOK A sip of the champagne Carlton's chef handed her. The bottle cost a couple hundred dollars, but the liquid felt caustic on her tongue.

Across from her, Marcos and Carlton clinked glasses, both smiling. Carlton was surely dreaming of the windfall he expected to come his way, Marcos silently gloating over being able to bring Carlton down soon. And even though Carlton had finished discussing business with Marcos and then made her an offer that she could try to build a case on, she didn't feel any cause for celebration. All she felt was slightly ill.

Morning had rapidly passed, and no matter how many hints she'd dropped about needing to head out, Carlton wasn't letting her go anywhere. It had been six hours since Jesse had stumbled into the wilderness, bleeding and alone. Was he already dead? Even if he wasn't, did she have any chance of finding him? The fact was, simply following her own tracks back to civilization was going to take all of her concentration. Carlton's mansion was purposely well off the beaten trail. And by the time she made the long drive back to the station for help, chances were the temperatures would be down below twenty. How long could Jesse hold out, even if they could locate him?

"Don't you like the bubbly?" Carlton asked. "This is from my private collection."

She forced a smile. "It's very good. But I really should leave soon. I don't want to be navigating the Appalachian roads in the dark."

Carlton gave her a slimy smile. "You could always wait until morning."

"No." She took a breath, tried to modulate her tone. "I've got work tomorrow. And I want to propose this new plan of ours, for helping kids make the transition out of foster care. I want to be at my best."

Carlton nodded soberly, and Brenna kicked herself for not using this excuse hours ago. She'd been so distracted by her fear for Jesse, by trying to hide her disgust for Carlton—even for Marcos—that she hadn't been thinking straight. Of course the best way to get Carlton to agree was to appeal to his own interests.

"That's a good point," Carlton said. "Finish your champagne, and I'll have my guards bring your car."

"We can get them," Marcos jumped in, so quickly Brenna frowned.

He'd been so determined to hang around

Carlton's place, dragging out their discussion for hours, that it was strange he suddenly wanted to go, too.

Carlton shrugged. "Suit yourself. My guards will take you out there, then. I'm not sharing the lock code with anyone."

Marcos seemed to pale a little and Brenna studied him, trying to figure out what was going on with him. But she shook it off; it didn't matter. All that mattered was getting back to the station and sending resources to find the kid wandering around the Appalachian Mountains before it was too late.

She tipped back the glass and drank her champagne in several long gulps. When she set it down, empty, Carlton laughed.

"Okay," he said. "Guess that means you're ready to pack your bags. I have to say—" he looked her up and down "—I'm a little disappointed. But you remember the lesson you learned today about betrayal, and everything will go just fine. I'll give you your security and you give me what I really need."

Brenna kept her jaw tightly locked and simply nodded. What he really thought he needed were more impressionable kids to do his bidding. Kids he figured were expendable. Kids he wouldn't hesitate to kill if they interfered with his plans. Just like Jesse.

"Don't be so sensitive," Carlton said, clearly not fooled by her attempt to hide her true feelings. "Just ask Marco here. Over time, you'll get used to it. And believe me, the money you'll get in return is more than worth it."

Tears pricked her eyes. Was that how Marcos felt about what he did? That trading the life of a kid who'd already made the wrong choices was a small price to pay to bring down someone like Carlton? Was that what she'd have to accept to do the same?

She didn't think she could. And she didn't want to become someone who was okay with that sort of trade. But where did that leave her?

Pull it together, Brenna told herself. She could figure out the rest of her life once she made it out of here.

"I'll be in touch tomorrow," she told Carlton, amazed that her voice actually sounded normal. "Expect good news about the program."

He grinned. "I knew I chose you for a reason."

She nodded, anxious to get out of there. She didn't look back as she hurried to her room to shove her belongings into the small bag she'd brought with her. She was practically running as she returned to the living room, ready to go to her car and get out of this soul-stealing place.

But she skidded to a halt when she reached

the living room, because instead of finding Carlton and Marcos happily sipping champagne like she'd left them, Carlton was fuming. And his guards were both pointing guns at Marcos.

She looked over at Carlton, her desperation turning into dread. "What's going on?"

"You tell me, *Officer* Hartwell."

Chapter Twelve

"What are you talking about?" Brenna demanded, a beat too late.

Not that it would have mattered if she'd denied it instantly. A minute after she'd left the room, Marcos had watched Carlton take a phone call. He'd glanced at the readout and then picked it up so quickly Marcos had known it was important. As the person on the other end spoke, Carlton's expression had gotten darker and darker, then his gaze had flicked to Marcos and he'd known the game was up.

Carlton knew the truth.

"You're a rookie," Carlton said now, sauntering over to Brenna, where she stood clutching a duffel bag and looking dangerously pale. "And your station let you come here?" He tilted his head, frowning. "You *are* a natural, I'll give you that."

Without warning, before Marcos could do

anything to stop it—not that he could with a guard locked on each arm—Carlton's fist shot out, catching Brenna under the chin.

Marcos yelled and tried to yank himself free, but the guards had a tight grip on him, and all he managed to do was wrench his shoulders in their sockets. On the other side of the room, Brenna's head snapped back and she went flying. She slammed into the wall and then slumped to the ground.

Fury and panic mingled as she lay there unmoving.

Carlton sidestepped the duffel bag she'd dropped and started to walk toward her again, an angry purpose in his stride.

Marcos ignored the throbbing in his shoulders, tensed his muscles and dropped to the ground. The action caught the guards by surprise and they jolted toward him, falling with him in a tumbled mass of arms and legs and guns.

Sweeping his legs out wildly, Marcos lurched toward the guard to his right, trying to grab his weapon. Before he could get free of the second guard, who'd wrapped his arms around Marcos's shoulders, trying to pin him in place, Carlton ran over and lifted his own pistol.

He shoved the barrel against Marcos's head and snarled, "Try it again."

Marcos froze, and he could actually see the struggle in Carlton's eyes. The man wanted to kill him right now but knew it wasn't smart.

Time seemed to move in slow motion. It felt like hours, but surely had been less than a minute until Carlton slowly backed away and his guards stood.

"Get up," Carlton demanded.

Marcos did as he was told, his gaze going to Brenna, who was still out cold on the ground. He couldn't tell how badly she was hurt, but he knew one thing: Brenna couldn't weigh more than 120 pounds, and Carlton had once been a semiprofessional boxer.

He kept his hands up, submissive, willing Carlton to control his temper, praying Jesse had already gotten away. That the DEA would burst through the doors any second. That Brenna would open her eyes and tell him she was fine.

But it was all wishful thinking, and he knew it. He had no idea how Carlton had discovered the truth, but the drug lord had shown him the images someone had texted him: Brenna in police blues, out on the street, and him in a DEA jacket at a crime scene. Whoever Carlton's contact was, he had inside access. *Too* inside, because although Brenna had been using her own name, Marcos wasn't. And yet, Carlton had gotten off that call, looked him in the eyes and said, "Well, *Special Agent* Marcos Costa, after I kill you, I'm going to find your *actual* family and take care of them, too."

Marcos wanted to believe it was a bluff meant to scare him more than his own impending death. He wanted to believe that the fact that Cole and Andre didn't share his last name, weren't genetically related, would keep them safe. But Carlton had proved his source was way too good. And Marcos already knew he was a killer.

In that instant, he wished he could take back every decision he'd made in the past few months. He'd come here with noble intentions: to get a dangerous drug lord off the street. He'd known—and accepted—the dangers to himself. But *never* would he have done it if he'd thought he'd be putting his brothers—or Brenna—in danger.

Now they were all in the crosshairs of a killer. And it was entirely his fault.

IT FELT LIKE fireworks were going off inside her brain, each one bouncing off her skull before exploding. Brenna squeezed her eyes shut tighter, fighting the pain, when her whole body seemed to slam into something metal, then slide into a warm body.

A warm, *familiar* body.

She struggled for consciousness. Ignoring the new pain it caused, she forced her eyes open, but that didn't change the darkness. Panic threatened, and then Marcos—the warm body pressed against her—whispered, "Brenna? Are you okay?"

He sounded both relieved and worried, and she resisted the urge to press closer to him and give in to the blackness threatening again.

Instead, she tried to get her bearings and figure out what had happened. She remembered Carlton striding toward her. She'd felt rooted in place with shock, and then it was too late. She'd barely even seen his fist coming and then it had landed. The pain had been instantaneous and intense. After that...nothing but blackness.

"Where are we?" She thought she was whispering, but her head protested like she'd screamed the words. She tasted blood and realized she'd bitten hard on her tongue when she'd taken the hit.

"We're in a covered truck bed. It belongs to one of Carlton's guards," Marcos whispered.

Now that he said it, Brenna realized they were moving—it wasn't just her own nausea. The ground underneath them was bumpy, and whoever was driving wasn't trying to avoid a rough ride. She also realized why she was pressed between Marcos and the cold metal of the side of the truck bed. He was trying to keep her from further injury.

She tried to move around and discovered her hands were tied behind her back. Panic threatened anew, and Marcos shifted even closer to her, probably sensing it.

How he could control his movements at all, she wasn't sure. As much as she tried to hold herself in place, whenever the truck took a turn, she slid forward or backward. Without her hands free to brace herself, all she could do was hope she didn't hit too hard. Or that the impact wouldn't roll her over entirely. Because she wasn't sure she could take another bump to her face, no matter how small.

"Where are they taking us?" It was a stupid question; it was obvious Carlton wanted them dead. Knowing how or where wasn't going to change anything.

She struggled against the rope around her wrists, but her frantic movements just gave her rope burn and made her shoulders ache. Her breathing came faster, and she knew she was on the verge of hyperventilating.

"Try to breathe slowly. Relax," Marcos said in the same calm tone, and she wanted to scream at him.

How was she supposed to relax when a drug lord's thugs were about to kill them? But she closed her eyes and tried, breathing in frigid air through her nose until her pulse calmed. When she felt marginally in control again, she asked, "How long have we been driving? And how long was I out?"

"You were probably only unconscious for five minutes before they moved us to the truck. At first, Carlton was going to use my own idea against me and send us out into the Appalachians like Jesse."

Before he could say more, Brenna blurted what she'd been thinking ever since he'd suggested it that morning, "Wasn't there some other way? You sent the kid off to die."

"I gave him my car keys, Brenna," Marcos told her. "And when the guards took us to the outbuilding, my car was gone. He got the message. Hopefully, he's made it out of the mountains by now. If we're really lucky, the DEA has already found him and they're on their way up here. But Carlton and his chef took another car and headed down the mountain to try to intercept him. Carlton sent us with his guards instead of just leaving us to wander the wilderness."

Brenna let the information about Jesse sink in, and relief followed. She tried not to dwell on the part about where they were going.

"You really thought I'd just let Jesse die?"

"I thought it was the only option you saw," Brenna replied, but she felt guilty, because even though her words were true, she *had* thought it. That, given the impossible option of him or Jesse, Marcos had chosen himself.

"It's not ideal, I admit it. And I don't think Carlton realizes I gave him the keys. He seemed to think Jesse had hot-wired it on his own, but that's why we're here. He'd figured Jesse had no shot, and he wasn't about to take that chance with us."

"No," Brenna whispered. Of course he wouldn't. He'd discovered their true identities—she still didn't know how—so the only option was for them to disappear, with no way to tie it back to him. Which meant wherever the guards were taking them, Carlton figured no one would ever find their bodies.

That depressing thought had barely taken shape when the truck pulled to a stop and doors slammed from the front cab.

Brenna renewed her efforts to loosen the ties on her wrists, rubbing them frantically against a rough spot in the truck bed, but it was far too little and far too late.

The cover over the truck bed was pulled back and the guards stared down at them, wearing furious expressions and pointing semiautomatic weapons at their heads.

"Get out," one of the guards said, and the other grabbed her by the elbow and pulled her to a sitting position.

The world around her tilted and spun, and when it finally settled, she glanced around. Nothing but trees as far as she could see to her right. And when she looked left…terror lodged in her throat.

A sharp drop off the side of the mountain.

Chapter Thirteen

They were out of time.

Marcos locked his hands together behind his back as he climbed awkwardly out of the truck. Somehow, it was even colder here than inside that truck bed, lying on the cold metal. Wind whipped around him, raising goose bumps all over his body. Or maybe that was due to their current predicament.

He'd managed to saw the ropes against a rusted-out spot in the truck bed, fraying them enough while they'd driven that he thought a hard yank might break them the rest of the way. Not that it mattered with two guards, each holding semiautomatic weapons.

Behind him, Brenna was trying—and failing—to climb out of the truck bed by herself. She was hunched over the edge, one leg dangling down, her face pressed to the metal like she was trying not to throw up.

One of the guards swore and went to yank her the rest of the way when the second one warned, "Don't. You want her puking on you? Wait a second unless you want to burn your clothes when we get out of here. Carlton said not to bring any DNA back with us."

Stay calm, Marcos reminded himself, standing beside the truck, pasting a dazed expression on his own face and hoping they'd think he was disoriented from the rough ride. He was closer to the tree line; Brenna was closer to the edge of the cliff. He wanted to step toward her, terrified one of those guards was going to just give her a hard shove and send her over.

But he didn't move, because he knew any fast movement on his part might cause them to do the same thing. Instead, he spoke. "You drive us out of here instead, and the DEA will pay a hefty reward."

The guards looked at each other and laughed, but Marcos had already known it was a losing play. He just wanted their attention off Brenna long enough for her to move on her own—preferably closer to him.

And finally, she did. She took a deep breath and hauled herself the rest of the way out of the truck bed, stumbling over and then slumping to the ground beside him.

"Shouldn't have messed with Carlton," one

of the guards mocked her, striding over and putting his face near hers.

Marcos's pulse picked up. The guards were just like Carlton. And they were high on their new roles as his first line of defense since Carlton and Brenna had taken out the others.

He purposely didn't look at the second guard, just addressed the one leaning over Brenna. "Come on, man. He outweighs her by at least double. That wasn't exactly a fair fight."

Get closer, he silently willed the second guard, even as he tried to fight with his bonds behind his back. He kept his movements small, not wanting to alert them to what he was doing. But if Carlton wanted no DNA, that meant he probably didn't want them shot. No chance of blood splatter if they just jumped off the cliff on their own. Marcos was pretty sure that was the choice they'd be offered very soon: either jump or be filled with lead.

He needed to distract them long enough to give him a fighting chance. But even if he got his hands free, it was a long shot. Brenna was clearly out of the fight, hurt worse than he'd realized. And he was unarmed against two trained guards with weapons.

"No?" the guard continued to mock. "I guess all that police training is pretty useless, huh?" He nudged her side with the toe of his boot.

The second guard rolled his eyes and took a step closer. "Come on, let's get this over with."

The first guard smiled, a slimy grin that sent a different kind of fear through Marcos. "Don't you want to play a little before the kill?" He got down on his knees next to Brenna and took some of her hair between his fingers, sniffing it.

She turned her head a little, her lips trembling with a suppressed snarl as she pushed herself to her feet.

"Hey," the second guy said, grabbing his friend.

The first guard turned to shove him, and Marcos knew it was his moment. There was no time even for a quick prayer as he yanked his arms as hard as he could away from each other. There was a loud *rip* and then his hands were free.

"Watch out!" the first guard screamed, jumping backward and raising his weapon again.

Marcos leaped toward him, praying the second guard would spin to help and leave Brenna alone. He fell on top of the first guard, slapping the gun away from him.

It went off, a *boom* that sent the gun in an upward arc as the guard tried to control the kick and fight Marcos off at the same time.

Using the gun's momentum, Marcos shoved

it upward, slamming the weapon into the guard's face. He went down and Marcos hesitated, glancing backward. Continue fighting this one or go for the other?

Behind him, Brenna suddenly spun away from the second guard, as though she was going to make a run for it. The guard grinned, starting to lift his gun as Marcos screamed a warning and tried to leap on him.

Before he could, Brenna slammed her tied hands toward the guard and ran backward instead of forward, straight into him. Marcos saw a flash of metal—was that a *butter* knife?—then the guard screamed, and Marcos landed on top of him.

The guard had dropped the butt of his weapon in favor of clutching his bleeding leg, trying to pull out the butter knife Brenna had somehow lodged pretty far into his thigh. Marcos went for the gun dangling from the strap over his shoulder, but he knew he wouldn't get control of it fast enough.

The guard he'd dropped was getting up, lifting his own weapon, his finger sliding beneath the trigger.

Abandoning his plan to fight, Marcos spun away from them both and grabbed Brenna around the waist, redirecting her. Then he ran straight ahead, shoving her toward the downward sloping tree line.

Marcos picked up his pace. This was going to hurt, but hopefully not as much as a bullet.

The blast of one gun quickly became two as bullets whistled past, close enough for him to feel the displaced air. He increased his pace, his strides dangerously long in the slippery, dead leaves. Then his right foot lifted off the ground and didn't come back down onto anything solid again, and he was hurtling through the air, Brenna beside him.

ONE SECOND, SHE'D been running. The next second, there was nothing underneath her but air.

Brenna's stomach leaped into her throat, leaving no room for her to get a breath as she pinwheeled her legs uselessly. She yanked at the bonds holding her arms together, needing to get them free if she had any chance of bracing herself for the inevitable fall, but it was no use.

The ground came up at her hard and Brenna squeezed her eyes shut, curling into a ball at the last second. She slammed into the partially frozen ground, bounced off a tree and continued sliding down the steep hill.

It was better than the complete drop off the cliff in the other direction, but pain exploded behind Brenna's eyes at every jolt, reawakening the pain from Carlton's hit. Although she'd been playing up how badly she was hurt with the guards, it hadn't been far from the truth. It had been sheer will to survive—to make sure Marcos survived—that had given her the strength to jam the butter knife she'd hidden in her sock into the guard's leg.

She felt as if she bounced against every tree on that hill, like she was in a pinball machine, before she finally rolled to a stop at the bottom. Her vision still rolled along with the pain in her head.

"We have to move," Marcos said, and she tried, but when she attempted to get to her feet, she stumbled back to the ground.

Up felt like down and down, up. The attempt to stand sent everything spinning again.

In the distance, the shooting resumed, and bark kicked off a tree ten feet away. "Go," she managed to tell Marcos.

Instead, he picked her up, tossing her over his shoulder in a move that had her clenching her teeth to stop from throwing up. Then they were moving again, zigzagging through the forest, and all she could do was pray he held on to her.

It felt like hours, but Brenna was sure it was much less when Marcos finally stopped, lowering her carefully off his shoulder. Her whole body ached: her head, from Carlton's punch;

her stomach, from bouncing on Marcos's muscled shoulder; the rest of her, from bumping every tree on the hill. She couldn't keep from groaning at the bliss of lying still for a minute on the cold forest floor, dead leaves scratching her face.

Brenna focused on breathing without throwing up while Marcos went to work on the ropes around her wrists. A minute later, her hands tingled at the sudden rush of blood flow, and her hands were free. Her shoulders ached as she shifted awkwardly on her side, getting them in a more comfortable position. Her eyes were still closed, but she could see her pulse pounding underneath her eyelids.

"How are you doing?" Marcos asked, his voice soft with concern as he brushed hair out of her eyes.

"I'm alive," she groaned, then cracked her eyes open, testing how badly it hurt. Realizing the trees actually blocked out a lot of the sun and that the world was settling around her, she opened them the rest of the way. "Did we lose them?"

"For the moment," Marcos answered. "But we'd better keep moving."

Brenna wanted to nod and climb to her feet, but everything hurt. She'd used the last of her reserves trying to take down the guard, and when she told her body to move, nothing happened.

"I think we can pause for a minute," Marcos finally said.

She closed her eyes again, wanting to just rest, and then he was lifting her carefully into his lap, tucking her head against his chest. His warmth seeped through her shirt, and she suddenly realized how cold she was.

Marcos's warmth seemed to replenish her strength, and Brenna sucked in a deep breath of the bitterly cold air. "You're right. We'd better go. If we get stuck out here overnight..."

He didn't finish her sentence, but he didn't have to. He had to know that if they were still here when the sun went down, their chances of surviving dropped even lower than the temperatures would.

Chapter Fourteen

Marcos glanced over at Brenna, trying to be subtle about it. He'd already asked her three times how she was doing since they'd started moving again, even offered to carry her again once. Each time, she'd responded in brief monosyllabic replies that made it clear she was doing this on her own.

But it wasn't her annoyance that concerned him. He knew she hadn't been short with him because she was mad; it was taking everything she had just to keep putting one foot in front of the other. He could see it in the tense way she gritted her jaw, in the careful steps, the glazed-over stare focused straight ahead.

She'd been unconscious for too many minutes after Carlton had punched her. Add the tumble down the hill, and he was worried her injuries were more dangerous than they appeared. He'd watched a friend in the DEA take a blow to the head and seemingly bounce back, only to die from it hours later. The idea of losing Brenna that way terrified him.

After all the years apart, he'd accepted that she was part of his past. That she was never going to be more than his first crush, and any imagining who she'd turned out to be was simple fantasy.

But now that she was in front of him again? The truth was, even though he barely knew her still, the fantasy couldn't even begin to compare with the reality. And he had a pretty vivid imagination.

Now, he was determined to do whatever it took to get them both out of this, so that he'd get a chance to really know her. To see if maybe they'd always been meant to have more than just a shared past.

Still, he respected her determination to survive this, to make it on her own. And the truth was, between bouncing down that hill and the beating he'd taken from Carlton's guards just yesterday, running with her for the few miles earlier had taken a lot out of him. He could probably carry her again for a while, but he wasn't sure how long. All he knew was, it wouldn't be long enough to make it back to civilization.

He glanced up at the setting sun. It had to be

closing in on 5:00 p.m. now, and the sky was streaked in pinks and purples. Over the fiery shades of orange and red in the trees, it was gorgeous, but the sight made fear ball up in his gut. They weren't going to make it out of here before nightfall.

And as dangerous as the Appalachians were in the day, they were a thousand times worse in the dark. Especially with no flashlights to lead their way.

"We'd better look for a place to hunker down for the night soon." He finally spoke what he'd been thinking for the past hour.

Brenna slowed to a stop, turning to face him. "Shouldn't we push on? Those guards are still out there, still hunting us."

"Yeah, well, one of them is limping now." He stared at her, leaning close until a shaky smile stretched her lips.

"What are you doing?"

"Checking your pupils." Thank goodness, they looked normal. He reached out and stroked his fingers carefully over her cheeks to the back of her head, searching for another bump from when she'd slammed into the wall.

She went completely still as he probed the back of her head, discovering a small goose egg. "Does that hurt?" he asked.

"No," she whispered, staring up at him, her lips slightly parted.

He pulled back quickly. "Good. And your vision is okay?"

She threaded her hand in his, and his pulse picked up at how right it felt. It was ridiculous, given their situation, but he couldn't help it.

"Yes, I'm okay. I have a killer headache, but my vision is back to normal. I haven't thrown up or lost consciousness again. I'm okay."

He nodded, recognizing that she was listing the possible signs of a concussion. "Yeah, well, you were out for a while in the truck." He squeezed her hand and admitted, "You scared me."

She grinned. "None of this is a ball of laughs."

"True."

She looked skyward and bit her lip. "You're right. Wandering around in the dark probably isn't a good idea." Then her gaze swept the trees surrounding them, and he knew she had to be thinking about the animals that lived in these woods. "But are we any safer stopping? The guards might call it a night when it gets dark, but Carlton will probably have reinforcements by morning."

"We're at least a couple of miles east of Carlton's place now," Marcos told her.

"Really?" She let out a long breath. "I'm glad

you know that, because I feel like we could be wandering in circles for all I can tell. Any idea how far we are from getting out of here?"

"Too far," he replied, and she didn't look surprised.

"Let's see if we can put a little more distance between us and them," she suggested.

He nodded, letting go of her hand as they started up an incline. He stayed slightly behind her, in case she slid backward.

He knew there were houses out here, but he hadn't seen a single one since they'd run from the guards a few hours ago. Which was probably good—Carlton's money had purchased plenty of loyalty. If someone in a house *had* spotted them, chances were that they'd tell Carlton—or simply shoot on sight—rather than offer help.

It had been nothing but dense woods. Mostly they'd been traveling slowly downhill, but every once in a while, they'd have to climb up to go back down again. He'd seen a trail at one point, but avoided it. No sense walking a path where they'd be easier to spot.

So far, they'd been keeping a brisk enough pace to help warm them slightly, but Marcos knew it would be a whole different story once they found a spot to settle in for the night. He wondered if Brenna was right about them keeping moving.

"Hey," she asked, turning to face him, walking backward now. "Do you hear that? I think—"

Her words ended on a shriek, and she suddenly dropped out of his sight.

"Brenna!" He ran forward, and as he emerged at the top of the incline, he realized two things simultaneously: Brenna had heard the guards, whom he suddenly spotted in the distance off to the left, and they'd reached a summit.

Brenna had just dropped off the side of a cliff.

THE WIND SWALLOWED Brenna's scream as the ground disappeared beneath her, and then she was falling fast. Frantically, she grabbed for something, anything, and snagged a tree root.

The impact of holding it nearly yanked her shoulder out of its socket, but she squeezed tighter, her body swinging as she reached up with her other hand and held on with both. She took a few panicked breaths as her hands slipped a little…and then held.

Slowly, she looked down, and the vertigo she'd fought earlier struck again. This time, though, it wasn't because of the blow to her head. It was because solid ground seemed *miles* below her.

Holding tighter to the root and praying it wouldn't break, Brenna looked up. She'd fallen at least a foot off the edge of the cliff before she'd grabbed on to something. Above her, Marcos's terrified face came into view.

When he spotted her, instant relief rushed over his features, but new panic assailed her. Because off in the distance, she heard shooting. The guards had found them.

"Go," she told Marcos. "Run!" Maybe she could hang here until they passed, then find something else above this root to yank herself up with. But in the meantime, Marcos was right in the line of fire, an obvious target at the edge of a cliff.

She pushed off her disbelief, because it didn't matter now. What were the chances she'd turn just as the ground dropped away? Yeah, it was stupid, she realized now. She'd been cresting what she'd assumed was another hill. Not the top of a cliff. But the Appalachians were deceiving.

Instead of running, Marcos dropped flat on his stomach, and then he was dangling over the edge of the cliff, holding his hand out to her. "Give me your hand."

Brenna hesitated. Did he have hold of something with his other hand? Was he hanging too far off the edge to hold both their weight?

"Brenna!" Marcos insisted, his fingertips brushing hers.

The gunfire in the distance got closer, and now she could hear the guards yelling at each other, sounding triumphant.

Tightening her grip with her left hand, she hauled herself higher, reaching up with her right. And then she was soaring upward as Marcos hauled her over the edge like she weighed nothing.

As she crested the top, he hooked a hand in the waistband of her jeans and pulled her the rest of the way. She realized he *was* bracing himself with his other hand, using a tree he was lucky hadn't snapped with their combined weight. But there was no time to celebrate, because she could see the guards getting closer.

She started to get up, and Marcos pushed her back down, shoving her back the way they'd come, so she slid down the incline on her belly, making her body less of a target. She could hear him right behind her, and the guards coming from off to their left. Once the guards got to the edge of the cliff where she and Marcos had just been standing, they'd have a clear line of sight down below.

"Go," Marcos said as soon as she hit the bottom of the slope they'd just trekked up.

She lurched to her feet and ran, dodging trees and slipping in the dead leaves, only to regain her footing again. She had no goal, other than to run *away* from the bullets, but in the back of her mind, she realized she was probably heading straight back toward Carlton's mansion.

Changing direction, Brenna ran downhill instead of across. Her feet slid even more until she lost her balance. She caught herself on a tree, slowing, then took off again, trusting that Marcos was right behind her. She risked a glance backward and discovered that he was— in fact, he was *directly* behind her. As if he was trying to block her body from a bullet with his own.

How had she thought for a second that he'd let Jesse walk into the mountains to his death, without at least trying to do something? If she'd learned anything about this grown-up version of Marcos Costa, it was that he wasn't just brave. He was also smart. Every time they'd faced possible danger, instead of jumping to the gut reaction of fight or flight, he'd stayed in character and tried to reason his way out of it. Only when he'd absolutely had to had he fought.

And right now, if a bullet managed to find them through the trees, it would hit Marcos instead of her.

Brenna picked up her pace. Her feet barely seemed to touch ground and then they were up again, until she knew she was out of control, half falling down the incline and praying there wouldn't be another sudden drop-off ahead.

But it was working. She could still hear Marcos, staying on her heels. But the sounds of the gunshots were fading, and the guards' voices were distant now.

"Zag," Marcos instructed.

"What?" She glanced back at him and would have run smack into a tree if he hadn't grabbed her arm, redirecting her.

She ran the way he indicated, panting. Now that the threat was less immediate, her adrenaline started to fade. She realized her legs were burning from running, and she could feel every bruise covering her body. It was getting harder and harder to see, and Brenna slowed a little.

Then, Marcos's hand was on her arm again, and he pulled her to a stop. "I think we lost them."

He sounded out of breath, too, and he rested his arms on his thighs, just breathing heavily for a moment.

She leaned against the tree and did the same, watching him. He hadn't left her. Not that she'd expected him to, even when she was telling him to go. But she'd needed to at least try.

"You could have left me."

He swore and straightened. "Not a chance. We're a team, remember?"

"Yeah." She palmed his cheek, running her fingers over the scruff starting to come in. It was so dark against his pale skin, and the contrast fascinated her for some reason. Or maybe it was just the man who fascinated her. The truth was, he always had.

He pulled away. "We should keep moving, try to get a bit more distance from the guards."

"You still hear them?" She strained to listen.

"No, but I don't want to take any chances. I doubt we have more than twenty minutes before we're completely out of light. So, let's get as far as we can and then find a spot to hunker down for the night."

Brenna glanced around her. As far as she could see, everything was the same. Towering trees with bare branches that cast ominous shadows in the semidarkness. Slippery leaves underfoot. In the distance—the opposite direction she knew the guards were—a big branch snapped, making her jump.

What animals were out here in the mountains? Bears, for sure. Maybe wolves?

Brenna shivered and moved forward, a little more cautiously, Marcos right behind her, as the night grew blacker and blacker around them.

Chapter Fifteen

Under any other circumstances, huddled in the dark with Brenna Hartwell sitting between his legs, her back against his chest and her head tucked under his chin, would be heaven.

Marcos had done the best he could, imitating what he'd seen his brother Andre do in practice before: camouflage them with their natural surroundings. Andre worked for the FBI as a sniper, but he'd trained with the military's best Special Operations groups, and he could make a hide pretty much anywhere.

Without Andre's training, Marcos knew his hidey-hole wasn't perfect. But ten minutes before the light would be completely gone, he'd pulled Brenna to a stop beside a huge, fallen fir tree. After checking carefully to verify that no animal had already claimed it, he went to work creating a space underneath it for them to wait out the night. He'd layered fir branches as a pseudo-carpet, to keep them off the cold ground. Then, he'd piled more tree branches around it, hoping to keep in as much warmth as possible, knowing the temperatures were supposed to drop well below freezing overnight.

Neither of them was dressed for it. He was slightly better off than she was, in jeans and a crew-neck wool sweater. Brenna had topped her jeans off with a lightweight T-shirt. Huddling close together and sharing their body heat was the smart move, but the feel of her body against his was distracting. Being in the dark, not being able to see her, seemed to make him hyperaware to every tiny movement she made.

"How are you feeling?" he whispered.

They'd been silent for the past twenty minutes, listening to a pair of owls that had claimed a spot somewhere in the trees above them. They hadn't heard the guards, but Marcos figured they'd returned to the mansion and would regroup in the morning. Which meant he and Brenna needed to start out again at first light.

"I'm fine," she whispered back, sounding like she was trying to be patient with his new favorite question.

Chances were slim that the guards were still searching, but they were keeping their voices low just in case. Especially since there was the possibility the guards would be afraid to return to face Carlton's wrath without having taken care of them for good.

"We should try to get some sleep," he told her, but ruined his own plan when a minute later, he couldn't help but ask, "What's your life like now, Brenna?"

He'd been wondering ever since he'd realized her true identity. Most of what he knew about her came from those few months when she was eleven years old. Although he'd tried to get close to her then, it had been in the innocent ways of a boy with a crush, and he'd mostly tried to support her in her grief.

During the five years he'd lived in that foster home with Cole and Andre, other kids had come and gone. The two boys who'd also lived there during the time of the fire he'd barely known more than the Pikes' biological son, Trent—grown and long gone before he'd moved in. But Brenna had always been different, and he didn't think a year had gone by since then that he hadn't wondered what she was doing.

It was hard to imagine the little Brenna Hartwell he'd known growing up to become a cop, and yet, somehow it seemed perfectly natural. The picture Carlton had flashed on his phone of Brenna wearing her police blues, looking so serious and focused, was such a contrast to the woman who'd attacked a guard to save his life, to the woman who'd melted in his arms that first night. He wanted to know all the different sides to her, and he was certain he'd only scratched the surface.

She shifted a little, the outsides of her thighs rubbing the inside of his. He looped his arms around her waist, holding her still, pretending he was just trying to keep her warm.

"What do you mean?" She sounded tentative, like maybe she didn't want to discuss real life with him.

But there was no need for cover stories anymore, and although he'd seen plenty of glimpses of the real Brenna, he wanted to know more. A lot more.

"What's your life like when you're not out here in a drug lord's house, playing a role?"

"I don't know."

She squirmed a little more until he laughed and told her, "You've got to stop doing that."

"Oh." He didn't need to be able to see her to sense her flush. "Sorry."

"Okay, I'll start," he said. "I work out of the DEA's district office in West Virginia. I've been there about five years, joined pretty soon after I finished school."

He paused, remembering the guilt he'd felt when he'd first started college. He'd wanted to go so badly, had been willing to work to put himself through, but his oldest brother Cole had insisted he focus on school. So while Marcos had worked part-time, Cole had taken on two jobs. Both Marcos and Andre had gone to college, while Cole had worked to make sure they had the life they might have gotten if they'd grown up under normal circumstances, instead of foster care.

"Where'd you go just now?" Brenna asked.

"Just thinking about how lucky I got. The day I turned eighteen, Cole had a home waiting for me."

Her fingers twined with his in her lap. They were icy cold, and he held tight, trying to warm them.

"Most kids in foster care just suddenly end up on the street. Even though they've known it's been coming, they don't have a plan," she said. "But it doesn't surprise me what Cole did for you and Andre. Cole was always looking after everyone. And I might have only known you a few months, Marcos, but I know that even without him and Andre, you would have ended up somewhere like the DEA."

"Maybe. But what about you?"

"No one was waiting for me."

He'd expected as much, from some of the things she'd said in Carlton's mansion, but the thought physically pained him. He wished he could rewind eleven years and be standing on her porch the way Cole had been standing on his the day she'd turned eighteen. Except he hadn't known where she'd ended up. And the truth was, he'd been afraid to look, afraid where she might have gone after that fire, how she might have turned out. It was easier to imagine her happy than risk finding her not.

"You're sitting there feeling guilty about that, aren't you?" she asked incredulously. "I didn't come looking for you either, Marcos. We only knew each other for a few months."

"Yeah, but I never forgot you."

His words hung in the air a long moment before she replied softly, "I never forgot you, either."

BRENNA JOLTED AWAKE, freezing and disoriented.

Slowly, awareness returned: the scent of pine and old leaves surrounding her; the heat of Marcos's body against her back; blackness so complete she wasn't completely sure her eyes were open. Then, she realized what had woken her: branches cracking.

She twitched as the sound came again, and Marcos's breath whispered across her neck, then his arms closed tighter around her. "Deer," he said softly.

"Are you sure?" Her voice was so low it

could barely be called a whisper, but somehow he heard her.

"Yeah. I peeked through the branches a minute ago. There's a little family of them."

She relaxed against him. "How can you see anything?"

"It's darker in here than when you look out. There are some stars."

"Enough to see a trail by? Maybe we should start moving again." She knew if the guards weren't still out there searching, they'd be looking again by morning light. And she was pretty sure that she'd actually run closer to Carlton's mansion when they were trying to escape the gunfire last night.

Realizing she'd lost all sense of time, she asked, "Is it still night?"

"Yeah, you slept about four hours."

"Did you sleep?"

"Some."

She had a feeling that meant only enough to rest his eyes for a few minutes and keep watch the remainder of the time. "We can take turns, you know."

"I'm not worried about Carlton's guards. I may not make the world's best hide, but it's good enough to fool those two. If they're still out there, they're not close by. But I think we should stay where we are for now. If you're cold in here, it's a good ten degrees colder outside."

We are *outside*, she wanted to say. But the truth was, the canopy of branches did give the illusion of being indoors. If indoors had a broken heater. She couldn't stop the shiver that worked through her, and Marcos pressed his arms and legs closer to her.

"Aren't you cold?" she asked.

"Yeah."

"You don't seem cold." In fact, compared to her, he felt downright toasty.

"I'm keeping warm imagining the two of us being back at my house, with the heat blasting on high."

His house. "What's that like?" Even as she asked it, she realized it was unfair to probe into his life when she hadn't been willing to tell him about hers.

Not giving him time to answer, she said, "Never mind. None of my business."

"It is if you want it to be," Marcos said softly, making her intensely aware of the hardness of his chest against her back, the muscled thighs pressed tightly to hers.

Brenna couldn't stop herself from tensing, and there was no way he wouldn't feel it, the way they were pressed so closely together. Did she want Marcos Costa to be her business?

Probably more than she'd wanted almost anything else in her life.

But the Marcos of her fantasies wasn't the real thing. The man behind her was way more complicated, way more terrifying to her heart than she could have imagined. Because a fantasy she could hold on to all her life, a stabilizing force in a world she couldn't control, was one thing. Taking a chance on the real man and risking failure? She wasn't sure she could handle that.

Especially not now, when—even if they made it out of the mountains alive—her future seemed murky once again. Did she really belong in police work? Even though Marcos had made the choice that gave Jesse the best chance of survival, the question remained about her. Would undercover work—would any kind of work that involved regularly dealing with someone like Carlton Wayne White—change her in ways she didn't want to be changed?

She felt lost, not unlike the way she'd felt when that foster home had burned down all those years ago, or when the woman from Child and Family Services had showed up at the hospital a few months before that, right after her mother had died, telling Brenna she was going into the system. Over the years, she'd learned how to be alone. It was isolating, yes, but it was safe, too.

In some of those foster homes, it was the only way to survive unharmed. In others, she'd sensed a chance to make real friends, maybe even another person to consider family the way Marcos had found with Cole and Andre. But she'd never reached out, never taken that step, because it was too risky. And, if she was being honest with herself, even the idea had felt somehow like a betrayal to the mom who had done her best for Brenna, whose only failure was dying in that car without her.

The thought jolted her. Did she really think, all these years later, she should have died beside her mom in that car? Tears pricked the backs of her eyes, because she honestly wasn't sure. She missed her mom every day, but it hit now with a strength similar to the days after it had happened.

Was she willing to let anyone into her life? Willing to risk losing them? Even if that someone was the man she'd dreamed of since she was eleven years old?

"You're awfully quiet," Marcos said, making Brenna realize she let his statement go unanswered far too long.

Before she could figure out what to say, he continued. "We don't need to figure anything out here. How about this? You tell me about your place, and I'll tell you about mine. That's not too hard, right?"

"It's not about the house," she said, and cursed the crack in her voice.

"I know," he said softly. "You probably think that because I found Cole and Andre, my experience was really different than yours. And you're right."

She started to speak, but he kept going. "For five years, Cole and Andre and I were inseparable. And even after that house burned down and we were split up, in my heart I knew I was just biding time until each of us hit eighteen and we were back together. But I came to that house when I was seven. I was in foster care since I was born. They always say that babies have a better chance of being adopted, but when I was little, I had some issues with my heart. Gone now, but by the time they realized it wasn't a major issue, I was getting older. No one wanted me."

She tightened her hold on his hands, hurting for the little boy who probably hadn't understood why he didn't have a real family.

He was right about their experiences being different. She might have spent her life since her mom died feeling totally alone in the world, but that's how he'd entered it.

They'd chosen different paths. He'd let Andre and Cole in, made his own family when he'd had none. And she'd pushed everyone away, because she was too afraid of losing them to give anyone a chance. Maybe it was time to finally change that.

"I want you," she whispered.

Chapter Sixteen

I want you.

Brenna's words from a few hours earlier rattled around in Marcos's brain as he held her hand tightly in his, grabbing tree trunks for stability with his other hand as they picked their way down a steep incline. Snow had started falling sometime after she'd said those words, and now the ground was slick and he could see his breath.

She'd gone silent after that, and he hadn't pushed her, because he'd sensed in the tone of her voice that something important had just changed. Instead, he'd just held her, and eventually she'd drifted back off to sleep. He'd woken her a few hours later, battling his fears of venturing back out into the cold or waiting until it warmed up a little more and risking Carlton sending reinforcements on the mountain.

They'd been up now for a few hours, moving

at a brisk jog most of the time. But this incline was slippery enough with the light snowfall that they were moving more carefully. The sun was starting to come up, and he'd been hoping it would bring warmth, but instead, the sky was hazy, threatening more snow. He prayed they were going the right way; his internal sense of direction was usually good, but they'd definitely veered off course running from the guards last night.

"We have to be getting close," Brenna said, every word puffing clouds of white into the air. Her cheeks and nose were bright red, and her fingers felt like icicles in his.

He'd stopped feeling his toes an hour ago, which made him worry how she was faring in her much lighter top. But whenever he'd asked, she'd given him a patient-looking smile and told him she was a skier and used to the cold.

"Yeah, I hope we're close," Marcos replied. The truth was, if they didn't emerge from the forest and onto flat ground soon, he was going to worry that this off-the-trail route he'd picked out for them wasn't as straight a shot as staying on the road. Of course, they couldn't stay on the road or they'd risk running right into Carlton. And while he hoped the DEA was also on that road by now, he didn't want to take the chance.

"You're a worrier," Brenna said.

"This seems like a good time to worry." He kept the rest of it to himself. He was mostly worried about *her*, that she was warm enough, that her head was okay after the hit she'd taken yesterday.

"Well, sure. But I feel a lot safer right now with you than I did in that mansion with Carlton." He must have still looked concerned, because she squeezed his hand and added, "We have to be close. Once we make it to civilization, then we worry about bringing down Carlton."

"I'm hoping the DEA is already there, and he's in handcuffs. Because if they didn't get the message and Carlton hasn't found us..."

"He's going to run."

"It's his best bet. He assaulted a police officer and a DEA agent—and killed one of his own guards in front of us. Besides, I heard him order his guards to kill us, so he can claim all he likes that they acted alone, but his testimony isn't going to sound better than mine."

Brenna picked up the pace. "Then let's make sure we beat him."

Her feet started to slide out from underneath her and he gripped the tree trunk, pulling her back toward him before she fell in the snow. She grabbed his shoulder with her free hand to brace herself, and then they were pressed tightly together, reminding him of the first night he'd seen her.

He must have telegraphed what he was thinking with his eyes, because her eyes dilated. All of a sudden, he felt like he was the one whose world was sliding out from underneath him as she leaned up and pressed her lips to his.

Her lips were cold, and so was the tip of her nose as it pressed against his cheek, but his must have been the same, because she leaned back for a second and whispered, "You're cold."

Then her tongue was in his mouth, and he didn't feel cold at all. He let go of the tree trunk and wrapped his free hand around her waist, bringing her closer still. And somehow, even in the frigid mountains with a drug lord out to kill him, he knew he was exactly where he was supposed to be.

For a few blissful moments, he let himself forget everything else and just *feel*. The way her fingers curled into his shoulder. The way she arched toward him whenever his tongue stroked the inside of her lip. The strength of her body underneath his hand as he palmed her lower back. For a few moments, there was nothing but Brenna.

In some ways, he knew nothing about her. He had no idea how she drank her coffee, what she liked to read, where she saw herself in five years. In others, he knew her better than most of the people he saw every day: the pain she'd survived; her determination in her job; her compassion for those she tried to help.

And yet, it wasn't anywhere near enough. Not the little bit she'd let him into her world and not this amazing kiss with both of them in too many clothes and with too many secrets still between them. Because what did she really know about him, either? Once they got back to real life, would they have anything in common?

If the answer was no, he half wanted to stay exactly where they were, no matter the consequences.

As if she could read his mind, Brenna pulled back and echoed his words from the other night. "I tell you what, when we get out of here, you show me your place and I'll show you mine."

She spoke fast, as though if she didn't get it out quickly, she wouldn't say it at all, and Marcos nodded just as fast. "It's a deal."

Then he grabbed the tree in front of him, keeping a tight hold on Brenna with his other hand, and started moving again.

CIVILIZATION HAD TO be close.

Brenna had been thinking it for more than an hour and, as big snowflakes started to plop on her head, she finally gave in to the worry that something had gone wrong. That getting out of the mountains would take longer than they'd estimated. Because although she'd been telling Marcos otherwise for hours, the cold was starting to affect her.

Now, when she grabbed the trees they passed for stability, she had to squeeze a little tighter in order to feel the bark. Her fingers were getting clumsy and numb, and her shivering had become erratic and violent. It hadn't warmed up, though, and her mind was still sharp enough to know her body was beginning to shut down.

Glancing up at the sky as another fat snowflake landed on her face and then slid down her neck, Brenna frowned and gave voice to her fears. "I think a storm is coming."

"I know." Marcos sounded as worried as she felt. "We either need to find shelter now and wait it out, or press on and get to help."

She looked over at him, noticing that his lips were tinged just slightly blue. "We might not make it to help if it gets much colder."

"A hide isn't going to keep us much warmer," Marcos said. "I did my best last night, but I'm not sure we can risk stopping. If we stop moving, we're going to lose body heat."

"If this snow keeps up, we've got the same problem. It's going to soak us."

"Let's try—" Abruptly, Marcos cut off, then

pulled her another few steps forward, peering into the distance. "Is that—"

"A parking lot," Brenna realized. "And cars. Maybe someone will be there. Or there will be an emergency phone."

She moved faster, half speed-walking, half-sliding down the hill, Marcos's hand somehow still holding tight to hers. The descent felt only partly in her control, partly a dangerous slide she'd never come out of—much like her feelings for the man next to her.

Finally, they reached the bottom of the incline and Brenna might have cried tears of joy—except she was pretty sure they would have frozen the instant they touched her skin. The trees thinned out here, and then the end was finally in sight.

She glanced at Marcos, who was staring at the parking lot at the end of the expanse of woods with similar disbelief. He grinned at her, a full, dimpled smile that sent warmth back into her, and then they took off running.

Brenna had an instant flashback to being eleven years old. She'd been watching as Marcos, Cole, Andre and the other two kids in the foster home had played a game of touch football. They'd invited her, but she'd declined. Even after she'd healed from her injuries in the car crash, she'd felt like her world was in slow motion. Later, she'd recognized that she'd been in a deep depression, but at the time, she'd just felt dazed, unable to really connect with anyone around her.

Only Marcos had made her feel like she would ever come out of that daze. That day, in the middle of the game, he'd run over to the sidelines and handed her the football he'd just caught. Then he'd grabbed her hand and raced with her across the goal line. For a few brief moments, Brenna had felt her childhood return. She'd felt free, even happy.

The same feeling rose up now, and Brenna let out a joyful laugh. They were so close. She could see that the cars were empty, but there *was* an emergency phone, and it was in a little glass enclosure that would keep the wet snow off their faces and the wind off their backs. Then it would be a matter of half an hour— tops—and they'd be in a warm car and heading home.

And then what? she wondered, feeling her feet slow just a little. Would she and Marcos simply go their own ways? She'd invited him into her home—into her life—but soon, they'd have cases to finish, real life to resume. Even if he still wanted to take her up on her offer, would he like what he discovered?

Up in Carlton's mansion, she'd been playing a role. Although parts of the person she'd been pretending to be—someone who would take advantage of kids, who would work with a drug dealer—were despicable, other parts were who she *wished* she could be. Someone confident, the kind of woman who'd walk up to a man she hadn't seen in eighteen years and kiss him as if the next logical step was to yank him into her bed.

The real Brenna was different. More measured, careful about everything she did. Part of what appealed to her about police work were the rules and boundaries. And she sensed Marcos loved undercover work at the DEA for the exact opposite reasons. Would she measure up to whatever he expected her to be?

There was only one way to find out. As Marcos glanced at her questioningly, Brenna picked up her pace again, holding even tighter to his hand.

"Stop right there!"

The voice came out of nowhere and seemed to echo off the mountain behind them.

Brenna jumped and would have fallen if Marcos didn't have such a tight grip on her. Together, they spun, and disbelief and dread slumped her shoulders.

Carlton's guards had caught up to them.

Chapter Seventeen

No way were they going to die this close to freedom.

Marcos stared at the furious guards as they moved in, keeping their rifles leveled on him and Brenna. The anger on their faces was personal this time, and Marcos instantly knew why. Both of them were sporting shiners that matched the nasty bruise underneath Brenna's chin. Apparently, Carlton hadn't been happy when they'd returned last night and had to explain his and Brenna's escape. Not to mention the man Brenna had stabbed was limping, a little blood seeping through his camo pants.

"Very soon, you're going to wish we'd dropped you off that mountain last night," the guard who'd taunted Brenna after taking them out of the truck said darkly.

"That'll seem like a peaceful way to go compared to what Carlton will do to you," the other guard added, then gestured back up the mountain with his weapon. "Let's go."

"I don't think so," Marcos said, keeping hold of Brenna's hand and taking a step away from them, slightly closer to the parking lot.

"Don't move!" the second guard yelled as the first one moved quickly around to the other side, so they were bracketing him and Brenna.

"You try anything, and we'll shoot you right here," the guard near Brenna warned.

"Really?" Marcos asked, keeping his tone confident as he turned to face the guard closer to him—the one in charge, the one less focused on Brenna. "On camera? You think that's a good idea?"

"What camera?" the second guard demanded, even as the first one swore.

"In the parking lot," Marcos said. "Right above that emergency phone. It's meant to prevent car theft, but believe me, the cops who monitor it will be really interested in automatic gunfire."

"So, move," the first guard demanded.

Marcos took a step backward, and Brenna did the same. He felt her back press against his, and he didn't have to turn to know—she'd lifted her fists, just like him.

"Are you kidding?" the second guard mocked. "You don't stand a chance. We're the ones with weapons."

"Sure," Marcos agreed. "And you use them here, and you're going straight to jail. I'm not following you anywhere. You want to take us back to Carlton, you're going to have to drag us. And incidentally, I don't think Carlton will be happy if you take us out." He grinned, back in character. "I'm pretty sure he wants to do it himself now. Am I right?"

It was a desperate play, and he knew it. But it was probably his only play. Following the guards meant waiting for a time to attack and hope to overpower them a second time, and it was unlikely. They wouldn't be so easily surprised a second time, and the cold had sapped most of his strength. The fact was, he wasn't sure he and Brenna would even live through a trek back up the mountain.

The first guard snarled, glancing from him and Brenna back to his friend. "Guess we have no choice." He shrugged, but there was glee underneath it as he centered his weapon on Brenna's head. "The cops want to arrest me for this? They'll have to find me first."

"Let's do this," the second guard agreed, lifting his weapon on Marcos.

"Wait!" Brenna yelled, but they ignored her, nodding to one another.

Just before the guards' fingers depressed on the triggers, Marcos shoved Brenna to the ground.

BRENNA SHRIEKED AS she hit the wet ground and Marcos landed on top of her, knocking all the air from her lungs. It was only a temporary reprieve, and she knew it. Marcos had gambled—it had been their only option—but they'd both lost.

She'd never get the chance to figure out where this new connection with him was going. Never get to see his house, reconnect with his brothers, all grown up. Never get to see Marcos in real life, when he didn't have to spend half their time together playing a role. Never get to find out if the way she felt about him now was a leftover childhood crush or the real thing.

She braced herself for the feel of bullets, but instead, she heard cars screeching to a halt, and then voices shouting over each other. "DEA! Drop your weapons!"

Then the gunfire came, and dirt and snow smacked her in the face as some of those bullets struck too close to her. All she could do was curl up smaller, pray Marcos was unharmed on top of her, and wait.

As suddenly as it had started, it was over. Marcos was standing, pulling her to her feet and away from the guards, who were down for good. Red sprayed across the white snow, and Brenna fixated on it instead of looking at the guards as agents ran toward them.

A pair of agents confirmed the guards were dead, and then more agents were leading her and Marcos down to the parking lot, as if they were incapable of making it there themselves.

"You okay, man?" an older agent, wearing a DEA jacket, his hair more salt than pepper, asked Marcos.

"Now I am." Marcos pulled Brenna closer, and she realized she was wedged in the crook of his shoulder.

Odder still, she couldn't imagine being anywhere else right now.

The agent glanced from Marcos to her, then stripped off his jacket and wrapped it around her. "Let's get you in the car. Heat's still on," he told her, gesturing for Marcos to follow.

She glanced back at him, and he smiled at her. "Meet my partner, Jim Holohan. Jim, this is Brenna Hartwell. She's undercover with…" He frowned. "Which department, exactly?"

"Harrisburg, West Virginia."

"Long way from home," Jim commented,

opening the door and ushering her into the back of a sedan.

A contented sigh escaped the second she sat down. Although she suspected it would take hours for her to defrost, it was warm in here. Now that she wasn't standing, she realized just how exhausted she was. Hopefully, in a few minutes, she'd start to feel her fingers and toes again.

She started to scoot over for Marcos to join her, but Jim slammed the door behind her. "Hey." She rolled down the window.

"She's okay," Marcos told his partner.

Jim seemed a little skeptical, but he nodded at Marcos and the two of them hopped into the front seat.

"Did you find Jesse?" Marcos asked.

"Yeah. Gave us a good scare when we spotted him racing out of the mountains in your car. We got him some medical treatment, and he's under arrest. Technically, we're holding him because he was driving a DEA car without authorization, but as soon as we have something more to make it stick, we'll be adding charges related to the drug-running operations. Me and a few of the other agents went straight up to Carlton's mansion, but it was empty."

"He was gone?" Brenna asked, surprised.

"But his guards said they were taking us back to him."

Jim shrugged. "Our guess is he hasn't gone far. We're watching the airports, but a guy like that has resources."

"Are agents still there?" Marcos asked. "He's got a *lot* of filing cabinets."

Jim grimaced. "He *had* a lot of filing cabinets. Well, I guess he still does, but they've been totally emptied out. Security footage and computers are gone, too. Everything else, he left."

"You're kidding me," Marcos said. "How'd he do that so fast?"

Jim shrugged, then gripped Marcos's arm. "We're glad you're okay."

Brenna could tell the two of them were close. But she supposed that was to be expected; who wouldn't get along with Marcos?

"We had a couple of close calls." Marcos told him about being driven out into the wilderness and escaping.

"About this *we*," Jim said, glancing at her. "You want to tell me exactly what you were doing in Carlton Wayne White's mansion without giving us a heads-up?"

"We can get into all of that later," Marcos said softly.

"He's a known dealer. Anything to do with

him should have gone into our system," Jim insisted. "Her very presence could have gotten you killed!"

"Go easy," Marcos started, but Brenna spoke over him.

"My investigation wasn't about drugs. It was about murder. And it's not over."

SHE WAS HOME.

Brenna looked around her little bungalow. She'd lived here for almost a year, and it had always felt comfortable. A place to get away from the world and recharge, just her. It was the first place she'd actually owned, and she'd taken joy in painting the walls cheery colors, in picking out furniture she'd get to keep. She'd figured if she was really going to put down roots, it was time to stop living like she was still a part of the system, being hustled from one place to the next with her single duffel bag.

Back then, the only things she'd cared about were the belongings she'd managed to bring along from her real home. Pictures of her and her mom, her mom's locket, a cherished stuffed animal her dad had bought her when she was a baby, back before he'd taken off for good.

She'd always thought that the day she'd turned eighteen, she'd start collecting things that were really *hers*. Instead, she'd clung to that old life, something in her unable or unwilling to create anything that might be taken away from her.

But when she'd started this job, she'd decided to make a change. Real job. Real life.

Except now, looking around her, it felt empty. And she realized what was missing was Marcos.

She let out a burst of laughter to calm her raging emotions. That was ridiculous. In her entire life, she'd spent a few months with him. And only three and a half days of that time was as an adult.

It wasn't him she needed, she told herself as she sank into a big, cushy chair she'd bought because it was something her mom would have chosen. But maybe this was a wake-up call. It was time to stop living such an isolated life.

Even now, after almost being killed by a crazy drug lord, she was here, alone. The chief had offered her protection, but they'd both agreed it was probably unnecessary. Carlton was crazy, but crazy enough to seek revenge against an armed cop on her own turf when the whole force was looking for him and getting caught surely meant a life in jail? She felt safe enough, but for once, the isolation itself bothered her.

Sure, her chief had called to make sure she

was okay—and to find out what they had on Carlton. And her mentor at the station had called, too. Victor's call was a lot more genuine, and she knew if she hadn't insisted she wanted to be alone, he would have already been at her house with his wife and their four kids. The same was probably true of some of the other officers she worked with, but it had been second nature to insist she was fine by herself.

She'd always been a loner. She had friends at work, but not the kind of friends she spent a lot of time with outside the job. And away from work? She had a few friends, but it was hard to maintain friendships when you didn't stay long in one place.

She should shower and change, maybe even go into the station and come up with a plan to get Carlton before he disappeared for good. But as the sun had started to set on the day, she'd discovered she had no energy left.

Marcos's partner had driven both of them to the hospital to get checked out. No surprise, they'd both been close to hypothermia. Even now, her fingers and toes throbbed. But at least she could feel them again. The doctor hadn't seen any sign of a concussion on her, and Marcos hadn't suffered any internal issues that they could tell from his beating. They were both going to be fine. Yet she was antsy, like her entire world had been upset and she'd never really be fine again.

Or maybe she hadn't really been fine since she'd been eleven years old.

"You're being a drama queen," Brenna muttered, forcing herself out of the chair. She was starving, but first she needed a shower and then, if she didn't fall asleep, food was next on the agenda.

She kicked off her shoes as she headed to her bedroom, and as she was shimmying out of her jeans, she realized there was something in the pocket. Pulling out the crumpled piece of paper, Brenna's heart rate picked up.

She'd forgotten all about the page she'd ripped out of the top of Carlton's pad in his office. Hurrying to the kitchen in her T-shirt and underwear, Brenna grabbed a pencil and shaded carefully across the page, hoping...

"Yes!" Indentations were on the page, and as Brenna squinted at it, she realized it was a phone number.

She probably should have called it in to her chief, have him run it, but she didn't want to wait. Carlton was out there somewhere, probably looking for a way out of the country if he wasn't already gone. And although her plan had been to get some sleep and go into the office as early as possible, when Jim and Marcos had dropped her off, she'd had no real leads.

She'd watched Marcos's curious gaze take in the outside of her little bungalow and bitten her tongue instead of asking him to come in with her. She'd half hoped he would ask—take her up on the promise she'd made on the mountain—but he'd just given her a quick hug goodbye. He and Jim had already been talking about the case as they'd backed out of her driveway.

Shaking off the disappointment that hit all over again, Brenna grabbed the cell phone she hadn't bothered to take with her to Carlton's mansion—not only would she not get service up there, she didn't want him looking through it. With fingers that felt oversize and clumsy, she dialed the number from the paper and held her breath.

It only took two rings and then a woman answered. "Hello?

Brenna drew in a sharp breath as the woman repeated her greeting twice more, then finally hung up. Then she sank into a kitchen chair in disbelief.

She knew that voice. She knew who Carlton's contact in the foster system had been all these years.

Chapter Eighteen

"Brenna Hartwell? From the foster home? Seriously?"

Marcos wrapped the blanket he'd grabbed as soon as he'd gotten home more tightly around himself. It didn't seem to matter how high he cranked the heat or how many hours it had been since he'd left the mountains. He couldn't seem to get warm.

His older brother Andre was still staring at him in disbelief. His oldest brother, Cole, frowned, watching him huddle more deeply into the blanket.

"Yes, that Brenna," Marcos said. "She's an undercover cop." His brothers had arrived an hour ago, after he'd spent several hours with Jim at the DEA office going over the weekend at Carlton's mansion.

His colleagues were busy trying to track Carlton and getting his picture out to anyplace he might try to travel. Eventually, once Marcos had given all the details he could, he'd known as well as they did that there was no reason for him to stay. Nothing besides his burning desire to be the one to slap handcuffs on Carlton.

But he wouldn't be any good to anyone if he couldn't function, and so he'd made Jim promise to call if they got a solid lead and had his partner drop him at home. The entire drive, he'd been wishing Brenna was still beside him.

When they'd dropped her off at her cute little bungalow, he'd been shocked at how close they lived without realizing when he'd spent so many years wondering what had happened to her. He'd desperately wanted to tell Jim to forget the debrief and follow her inside. But time was essential if they wanted to find Carlton, and the truth was, if he'd followed Brenna inside, he'd be tempted to distract her from what she needed to be doing now too: resting and healing.

He hadn't expected to find his brothers waiting for him in his house, but he hadn't been surprised, either. When Jesse had shown up instead of him, the first thing Jim had done before racing up to the mansion was to call Cole and Andre, in case he'd contacted one of them. It wouldn't have been protocol, but Jim knew how close he was with his brothers. Besides,

Cole was a detective and Andre was FBI, so they definitely had the resources to help him.

For the past hour, though, they'd both been in pure overprotective brother mode. Only now that he'd gone through the whole story with them—leaving out certain details between him and Brenna—was their concern shifting into something else.

Andre grinned at him. "You don't even have to say it. I see it all over your face. You're in love with this girl as much now as you were when you were twelve."

"I don't think...that's not..." Marcos stumbled, actually feeling the flush climb up his cheeks. Of all the times to suddenly get warm, this was just going to feed Andre's teasing. And that was usually Marcos's job.

He'd gotten used to teasing his older brothers, both of whom had dived headfirst into relationships over the past few months. He didn't like being on the other side of it. And Andre's word choice...

"I only spent a few days with her," he blurted. He couldn't be in love with her. He barely knew her. Except this overpowering mix of emotions he felt every time he so much as heard her name sure seemed like more than a simple crush.

Even Cole, who rarely resorted to teasing,

was failing to hide his smile. "Well, at least now we know she didn't actually set that fire."

His words instantly changed the mood in the room, and his brothers got somber again.

"It sounds like it was just an accident, after all," Andre said.

"Yeah. It's still bugging me a little that Brenna was at Carlton's mansion because of what she thought she saw all those years ago, and now we know it wasn't our foster father."

"Well, are you sure?" Cole asked.

"Carlton talked about a woman as his contact."

"Maybe he was lying," Andre said.

Marcos slowly nodded. Carlton wasn't exactly a reliable source of information. There'd be no reason for him to lie about that and yet, the man was mercurial. Anyone who'd turn on a potential investor as fast as he had could easily lie about details of his operation just because he was paranoid. "Maybe."

"Maybe we should—" Cole started.

The ringing of Marcos's phone cut him off. He didn't recognize the number, but he picked up immediately, because he'd given Brenna his contact information before dropping her off. "Hello?"

"Marcos? It's Brenna."

"Brenna," he saw Andre mouth to Cole, and

he realized he'd started grinning as soon as he'd heard her voice. He blanked his expression, but it was too late. His brothers were both hiding laughter.

"I thought you'd be asleep by now," he blurted.

There was a long pause, and then she said, "Marcos, do you remember how I told you I found something in Carlton's second office?"

Marcos sat straighter, dropping hold of the blanket. "No. What did you find?"

"Just a piece of paper. Turns out there was the indentation of a phone number on it. I called the number and I recognized the person who answered."

"Who?" Marcos glanced at his brothers, who both leaned forward as he asked, "Was it our foster father?"

"No. It's a woman who works in the Child and Family Services Division—not the location where I was pretending to work, but I've met her while setting up my undercover role."

"She knew you were a cop?" Marcos interrupted. Could that be how their covers were blown?

"No. She thought I was who I told Carlton I was. But it fits. She's set to retire in a few months. Carlton was recruiting me to replace her."

"Okay, I'll let my partner know. He can bring this woman in. What's her name?"

"I just wanted to give you the heads-up first," Brenna said, a stubborn undercurrent to her voice. "I'm going to get my department involved."

"Brenna, why don't you let the DEA handle this? We have more resources, and we've been working the Carlton Wayne White case for years."

Across from him, his brothers both cringed and shook their heads at him, but he didn't need them to tell him Brenna wasn't going to like that suggestion. And he didn't care. When he'd seen her slam into that wall in Carlton's mansion and then slide to the floor unconscious, he'd never felt more powerless or afraid. He didn't want her anywhere near this.

"This is my case, too, Marcos," she said softly, angrily. "I'm not stepping aside."

He sighed, knowing it didn't matter what he said. She was going to stick to the case. And although he admired her for it, he also didn't want her doing it on her own.

"Tell you what. Why don't we join forces?" He pinched the bridge of his nose, wishing he could just keep her out of it, keep her safe. "Andre and Cole are at my house. Want to come over and figure out a plan?"

"I'll be there in twenty minutes."

"Brenna," he said quickly before she hung up.

"What?"

"What's this woman's name? The foster care connection?"

"Sara Lansky." Somehow, she must have heard his surprise in his silence, because she asked, "You know her?"

"I know the name," Marcos said grimly. "And you were right all along about our foster father. He is involved. Back when we lived in that foster home, he was having an affair with a Sara Lansky."

"Are you sure?"

"Yes. And it explains what Carlton said about his source not even knowing she was his source. It's because she wasn't. She was giving the information to our foster father. *He* was passing it on to Carlton."

His brothers both swore softly, and Brenna insisted, "Don't go anywhere without me. I'll be there soon."

Then she hung up and he stared back at his brothers, anger warming him faster than hours inside, almost faster than thinking about Brenna. He'd nearly died in that fire.

It didn't matter that the foster home had given him Cole and Andre. His foster father was going to pay for what he'd done.

SARA LANSKY. IF the woman hadn't had such a distinctive voice, low and gravelly from years of smoking, Brenna wouldn't have recognized her so quickly. She barely knew the woman, after all. But Marcos's words rang in her head.

It made sense. Not just the way their foster father had gotten the records back then, but also the secretive way he'd slip down the stairs to his office in the middle of the night. Probably to call this woman.

Brenna had barely slept during those months at the foster home with Marcos and his brothers. A side effect of grief was that she startled to attention at every little noise. Twice, she'd crept down the stairs after their foster father, to see what he'd been doing. Once, she'd heard him open the back door and talk angrily to someone she'd later learned was his only nonfoster son, Trent, already grown and living elsewhere. The other time, he'd gotten on the phone and the conversation had quickly turned to things that at eleven years old, she hadn't understood. Now, she realized it must have been Sara on the line.

But how had their foster father gotten connected with Carlton in the first place to be passing information to him?

Brenna paused in lathering her hair, leaning against the wall of the shower. She'd spent so many years knowing that something had been wrong with what their foster father was doing that night, and determined to figure out what it was. Once she'd suspected the connection to Carlton, she'd been so focused on finding a way to bring Carlton down, she'd never stopped to wonder how they'd met.

Their foster father had to be at least twenty years older than Carlton, probably more. Eighteen years ago, he'd lived in a lower middle-class neighborhood, working a blue collar job. Apparently, he'd been cheating on his wife, but he'd come home to her every night. To her and their six foster kids, crammed into two of the four tiny bedrooms—plus her, as the only girl, stuck in a converted walk-in closet. They'd kept the third bedroom a shrine to Trent in case he ever wanted to come home. While she'd been there, he never had.

She'd never seen any evidence that their foster father was using drugs. And she couldn't imagine that he'd met Carlton—then a semi-professional boxer—while at work at the factory. So, where?

Shivering, Brenna realized the water was starting to get cold, and she'd only planned to take a fast shower and change before heading to Marcos's place. She ran her hands through her hair, rinsing out the rest of the suds, then turned it off and stepped onto her rug as a soft noise sounded in the distance.

She froze, straining to listen. Was it her imagination?

After a minute of dripping onto her bathroom floor, attuned to any sound, Brenna let out a heavy breath and dried off. Grabbing a pair of jeans and a sweatshirt, she debated whether to waste time with makeup.

Just lipstick, she decided, swiping some bright red across her lips. As she was flipping the switch on her hair dryer, there was another sound, like something sliding softly across her kitchen floor.

Dropping the hair dryer, Brenna raced around her bed to the nightstand where she'd left her service pistol. From behind her, whoever was in her house must have realized she'd heard and no longer tried to be quiet. Footsteps pounded toward her, and the bedroom door was flung open.

Carlton stood in the doorway, looking larger than life in all black, his white-blond hair tied back, and fury in his eyes.

Brenna scrambled to open the drawer, then Carlton was on her. His massive hands closed around her shoulders, and he tossed her away from the table as if she weighed nothing.

She landed on the edge of the bed, then tumbled off the other side. Her body, already sore from running through the mountains, protested at the hard landing, but she pushed to her feet fast.

It didn't matter. He was already in front of her, blocking her exit.

He didn't have a weapon that she could see, but that didn't matter, either. Brenna knew what one hit from this man could do.

Holding up her hands in front of her, Brenna warned him, "If you're trying to silence me, it's too late. We've already found your real connection in foster care, and he's going to dismantle the whole thing."

Confusion passed over Carlton's face, then he shook it off. "It doesn't matter what you think you know. I'm not here to stop you from talking to your department." He cracked his knuckles. "We both know it's too late for that. I'm here to make you pay."

Chapter Nineteen

"How did you know about Sara Lansky?" Andre asked. "I don't remember her."

"Phone bills," Marcos replied, checking his watch again discreetly. It had been almost twenty minutes, and he was anxious to see Brenna again, even though his heart was telling him to keep her as far away from this case—and the danger—as possible. "Our foster mother was going through them one day. There were all these late-night calls to the same number. She'd circled it and written the name there."

"Did she confront him?" Cole asked.

Marcos shrugged. "I don't know. She saw me looking and covered them up, but by then, I'd realized what it meant."

"If you're right about this, then our foster father started giving Carlton information on foster kids eighteen years ago," Cole said.

"Yeah." Marcos considered what that meant. Eighteen years ago, Carlton had been just starting out, but he'd become a major player in the DC area pretty quickly. And that meant major money.

"They kept fostering after that house burned down," Andre spoke up. "I asked about them a few times over the years. I guess early on, I was hoping that they'd want us back. That the three of us would wind up back together."

Cole nodded. "I think we all hoped that."

"Did he keep working?" Marcos asked. "Maybe they just fostered so he'd have a connection to Sara."

Andre shrugged. "I always assumed so, but I don't know."

"Let's find out," Marcos said, booting up his laptop and doing a search. A minute later, he leaned back and frowned. "Huh."

"What?" Cole asked.

"I can't find anything for at least a decade. It doesn't look like he's at the factory anymore, and he hasn't been for a while."

"Did he move somewhere else?" Andre wondered.

"I can't tell," Marcos replied. "I somehow doubt the foster care system wouldn't get suspicious if he stopped working all of a sudden, but I don't see anything."

"Well, what about the fostering?" Cole asked. "Is he still doing it? Because I always got the feeling they went into it because their own son was so distant, not totally for the money."

"Yeah, me too, not that they really jumped into parenting," Marcos replied. His memories of that house had been happy because of Cole and Andre. The foster parents had just been there; not bad, not good. They'd put a roof over his head and food in his belly and not a lot else, though they'd been far better than some of the other homes he'd lived in over the years.

But he remembered when he'd first arrived, his foster mother talking about her son, Trent, who was grown and had been out of their house for five years. According to the stories, he'd been a genius, but a troublemaker who hung out with the wrong crowd. She'd spent so much energy trying to steer him in the right direction that once he was gone, she'd claimed she'd wanted a second chance. She'd also claimed she had nothing left to give.

Marcos had met Trent a handful of times over the years. He'd swing by for an hour or so, watch the foster kids with what looked like disdain, chat with his parents for a while, then head out again. With a son like that, it didn't surprise Marcos that they might want to try again, except they never really had.

"Maybe that was just an excuse," Marcos said. "Maybe she was in on it, too."

"I doubt it," Andre replied. "Not if the connection was through a woman he was having an affair with."

"Good point." Marcos glanced at his watch again and frowned.

Cole did the same. "Brenna should be here by now, shouldn't she?"

"I'm going to call her," Marcos said, already dialing. But it went straight to voice mail and a bad feeling came over him.

His brothers were already on their feet before Marcos realized he'd jumped up and grabbed his car keys.

Cole took them out of his hand. "I'll drive. You direct."

Marcos nodded his thanks, dread propelling him into a run. "Let's hurry."

ONE HIT AND it was all over. One hit and Carlton could knock her out and then kill her before she even had a chance to fight back.

Panic made Brenna breathe faster as Carlton took a slow step toward her, a gleam in his eyes that told her he was going to enjoy hurting her. She had good reflexes—her years in foster care, some in houses with abuse—had taught her to dodge a blow instinctively. But he'd boxed semiprofessionally, and he'd already proved his fists could be faster than her reflexes.

But up in his mansion, she hadn't been expecting the hit. Right now, she was.

"You shouldn't have let Marcos drop you off and drive away," Carlton mocked her. "Maybe then you would have stood a chance. But I appreciate you sticking around while I learned where he lives."

Brenna's lungs tensed up, panic making it hard to breathe. After he killed her, he was going after Marcos. She forced the distraction to the back of her mind, knowing it was why he'd told her. Not just to torture her even more, but to keep her unfocused, unbalanced.

He proved it when he darted toward her, fist-first. Instead of an uppercut to her chin like last time, he went for her chest. Apparently this time, he didn't want her out of the fight right away—he wanted her to suffer.

She jerked sideways quickly and his fist soared past her, surprise in his gaze. Brenna changed direction just as fast, punching wildly, one fist after the other, both aimed at his throat. The first one bounced off, but the second one scored a solid hit.

He made a choking sound and stumbled back a step, but he regrouped quickly, and she hadn't expected anything less. With a past as a boxer, he knew how to take a hit and keep coming. Surprise would only get her so far. She needed a plan, or a weapon. Something. Because eventually, she wouldn't dodge fast enough and he'd take her down—or he'd decide to use brute strength and barrel into her.

Now, he gazed at her with a mixture of surprise, anger and a hint of respect. He smiled, and it was like a cat that knew it had a mouse cornered, but wanted to play with it awhile before making the kill.

"Not bad," he told her, and the way his voice came out broken told her she'd scored a better hit than she'd thought. "But not good enough," he added and swung his fist again.

This time his hand glanced off her side, but she knew if she lived through this there'd be a sizable bruise. She leaped right, and like a bizarre dance, he shuffled to face her.

Frantic, she worked through her options. Her gun was too far away. The hair dryer was discarded on the floor, running on low heat. Maybe she could yank the cord up and around him? There was a snow globe on her dresser that might do some damage if she could smash it against the side of his head.

Carlton was swinging again before she could decide, and she jerked right, almost stumbling over the hair dryer cord. She caught herself on the dresser at the last second, and then he was swinging again, and she knew she wasn't going to avoid this one.

Brenna ducked anyway, praying to minimize the damage, but before his fist landed, a crash sounded from behind them, startling him into pausing midswing and glancing back.

Not wasting any time, Brenna yanked the snow globe off the dresser and slammed it into the side of his head. The glass broke, cutting her hand and slicing into his scalp, making him yelp, but he was already swinging back toward her, fury in his gaze.

Then Marcos was racing through her bedroom door, and he jumped onto Carlton's back, sending the drug lord to the ground. Two men were right behind Marcos, and despite the passing of eighteen years, Brenna recognized them. Cole and Andre.

Before Brenna could fully wrap her mind around the fact that Marcos was here, he, Cole and Andre had Carlton pinned to the ground. Andre slapped a pair of handcuffs onto the drug lord, and then Cole was on the phone, calling for backup.

Andre and Cole literally sat on Carlton to keep him from racing out the door, handcuffs and all, and Marcos gripped her by the upper arm, looking her over carefully. "Are you okay?"

"I'm fine." She stared back at him, still in disbelief that he was here, in her house. "How did you know?"

"You took too long to get to my house." He pulled her to him, wrapping her in a hug tight enough that it made her side—where Carlton had gotten in a glancing blow—twinge.

But she ignored it, because the pain was worth it to be in Marcos's arms. She rested her head against his chest and closed her eyes, feeling safe despite Carlton still thrashing around on her floor. Feeling content for the first time in years.

Behind them, Andre loudly cleared his throat. "Not to interrupt the reunion, but do you want to give us a little help here?"

Brenna pulled free of Marcos's embrace to discover even with Cole and Andre both shoving him to the ground, Carlton was thrashing around, trying to pull himself free.

Marcos rolled his eyes and went to join them, but Brenna scooted past him, jammed a knee between his brothers on Carlton's back and yanked his cuffed hands straight up behind him.

Carlton roared and went still, and Marcos grinned. "Guess you don't need my help after all."

Then sirens sounded, and DEA agents were

piling into her house and dragging Carlton off to their vehicle.

Brenna turned and stared at Marcos and his two brothers, all grown up. Cole and Andre weren't quite what she would have pictured, and yet, she'd recognized them instantly.

"It's good to see you, Brenna," Cole said.

"We've been hearing a lot about you tonight," Andre added, and then they were both hugging her.

It wasn't the sort of brief, polite hug you'd give someone after reconnecting, but a genuine hug, the kind you offered to family. Tears welled up in Brenna's eyes, and she blinked the moisture away before they stepped back.

"At least this is almost over," Marcos said. "With Carlton in custody and only his chef still in the wind from the mansion, now we just need to bring in his foster care connection. Then it will take some time, but the rest of his organization will begin to fall like dominoes."

"That's not all," Brenna said grimly.

"Why not?" Cole asked.

Brenna looked from Marcos to his brothers and back again. "When I told Carlton we were about to bring down his real foster care connection, he looked confused, like he didn't know who I meant."

"Maybe he just thought you meant someone working with Sara," Andre suggested.

Brenna shook her head. "No, I'm pretty sure he genuinely didn't know what I was talking about."

"He said that the foster care connection didn't even know she was his connection," Marcos reminded her. "Maybe he couldn't believe you'd really gotten on to our foster father." He looked pensive. "Although he obviously looked into your past. He knew you'd been in that house, since you specifically mentioned the fire as part of your cover. I'm surprised he wasn't suspicious from the beginning because of that."

"Maybe it's because he didn't know," Brenna replied.

"How could he not know?" Cole asked.

"I think he's the front man," Brenna answered, as the things that had been bothering her since she'd brought it up to Carlton suddenly fell into place. "I think someone else is the real mastermind."

Chapter Twenty

"Who do you think is the mastermind?" Marcos asked.

He and his brothers were sitting in Brenna's living room, and he couldn't stop himself from glancing around again. Just like her bedroom, it was painted with a bright pop of color. The furniture was bright and full of personality, too. It all felt like Brenna and yet, something was off, as if she wasn't fully settled in yet.

Her house was quiet now that his colleagues had cleared out, taking Carlton with them. Normally, Marcos would have insisted on going with them. He'd wanted to be involved in questioning the drug lord, but he knew his partner would do a good job. Jim had more than fifteen years of experience, and if anyone could get Carlton to spill everything, it was Jim.

Still, Marcos knew that wasn't going to be a quick process. He'd told Jim he was exhausted and needed rest. Jim had raised his eyebrows and glanced at Brenna, like he'd known there was more to Marcos staying away from the initial questioning. And he was right.

It didn't matter that the biggest threat to Brenna's safety was now behind bars. Because she shouldn't have been in danger in the first place. It was completely illogical for Carlton to venture anywhere near the home of an armed police officer when the entire law-enforcement community was searching for him. And right now, Marcos wasn't going to be at ease unless he had her in his sights.

The fact was, he wasn't sure he'd ever be at ease again whenever she was out of his sight.

The thought gave him pause. He was in law enforcement; he knew and accepted the risks he took every day. He knew and accepted those risks with both of his brothers. But the thought of Brenna out on the streets in her police blues, or undercover again, made his entire body clammy with fear.

He knew she was capable. Not as well trained as her department should have ensured before she was sent out on a mission that involved Carlton Wayne White, but she was resourceful and strong. So, why did the thought of her at risk make him want to follow her around?

Marcos glanced over at his brothers, realizing that for all their teasing earlier, they were right. He was falling in love with this woman. No, forget the *falling*. He'd already collapsed at her feet, and he'd probably never get up again.

When he swore under his breath, Brenna gave him a perplexed glance, but his brothers just smirked at him. They knew him too well, and Marcos could just bet they knew exactly what he'd realized.

He was in love with Brenna Hartwell. Now he just had to figure out what he was going to do about it.

"…knew," Brenna said, staring at him as if she expected a response.

"Sorry. What?" he asked, trying to shake himself out of his fog, to focus on truly closing this case instead of on how to convince Brenna to take a chance on him. In the mountains, she'd made a deal with him: she'd show him her house if he showed her his. She'd fulfilled her end of the bargain, intentionally or not. But there was no doubt she was wary of relationships; how did he deal with that? How did he come to terms with dating a woman in law enforcement, who put herself in as much danger as he did every single day? And how did he overcome what had always seemed to be his nature: to only stay in a relationship until it got too serious, and then bail before she could?

Because truth be told, he was wary of relationships, too, probably for the same reason she was.

"I said, I wish I knew," Brenna repeated. "Maybe it's our foster father?" She sounded unconvinced.

"We looked into him. It looks like he stopped working at the factory about a decade ago," Marcos told her. "I can't find anything about him working elsewhere, but I assume he was. We'll have to take a lot closer look, but if he was the mastermind, why let Carlton take on the front role? How would he have gotten hooked up with the guy?"

"I've been wondering that myself," she said, then shrugged. "I don't know. Maybe I'm wrong. Maybe Carlton was confused for some other reason, but my gut is telling me there's more here than we're seeing."

"Well, some of the things he said up in the mountains did make me wonder if either there was a second in command we don't know about making a power play, or if Carlton could actually be reporting to someone. If he really isn't the one in charge, then it's somebody pretty brilliant, because it's not just law enforcement who thinks so, but everyone I've talked to in the drug world. And I just don't see our foster father in that role."

"Maybe we need to pay Mr. Pike a visit," Cole suggested.

Andre looked at his watch. "It's almost three in the morning. Why don't we all get some sleep first? We can do it tomorrow after work."

"Or Brenna and I can go in the morning," Marcos suggested, his gaze darting to Brenna's bandaged hand. One of the EMTs who'd shown up with the DEA had stitched up Carlton's head and then wrapped her hand. It wasn't bad, but things could have been so much worse. He wanted to end this, stop any possible threat still out there as soon as possible.

His brothers didn't look thrilled about not being included, but Marcos didn't want to wait a full day. The fact was, he wanted to charge over to his foster father's house now, but Andre was right about it being a bad time to go knocking on someone's door if they wanted answers, especially when they had no proof of his involvement. And they didn't even know where he lived anymore.

"I wish I could skip out tomorrow and come with you," Cole said, "but I trust you'll keep us updated as soon as you know anything?"

"Of course," Brenna replied before Marcos could answer.

"Good," Andre said, standing and yawning. "Then let's head out. Brenna, you need a bag?"

Brenna stared up at him in confusion. "What?"

"You're staying with Marcos tonight," Cole answered for him. "Even if Carlton is behind bars, he cut a hole in your window that you need replaced. And we kicked down your door to get in. Yes, it's temporarily boarded, but you shouldn't be staying here like that."

"I'm armed," Brenna reminded them.

This time, Marcos didn't let his brothers speak. "You pick. Either you come stay with me or I stay here. But I have to warn you, given the fact that Carlton was here tonight and you think he's got someone pulling his strings, neither of us will sleep much if I stay here because Cole and Andre will be calling all night."

They both nodded, and she rolled her eyes. "All right. I'll get a bag, but you should know that Carlton must have found my place following us from the parking lot after his guards were taken out. He said he followed you back to your house before returning to mine. He was going to go after you next."

His brothers were instantly frowning again, and Marcos didn't want to drive out to either of their places, so he said, "Okay, we'll be extra cautious and check into a hotel for the night."

Brenna flushed at his words, and Marcos wished either of them were in any shape to do anything besides get a solid eight hours of sleep. But the hours on the mountains were catching up to him fast.

"You sure?" Andre asked. "Because I have room—"

"I'm sure," Marcos cut him off, then stared after Brenna as she disappeared into her room to pack an overnight bag.

And suddenly, he felt twelve years old again, meeting a little girl he was just sure he was going to marry someday.

BRENNA STARED AT the king-size bed in the center of the hotel room, and her heart did a little flip-flop. It didn't matter that she was too tired to do any of the things that instantly came to mind as Marcos sank onto the edge of that bed. And yet, instead of backing away like she should have, she found herself moving toward him.

His head lifted at her movement, those blue-gray eyes locking on her, hypnotizing. Then his arms were up, reaching for her, and she couldn't help herself from climbing onto his lap and wrapping her arms around his neck.

She'd expected him to pull her head to his, to lock their lips together, for passion to spark instantly like it had that first night she'd seen him. Instead, he gave her a soft smile and cupped her cheek, his thumb stroking her somehow more of a turn-on than full-body contact with any other man.

"You didn't answer your phone, and I don't think I've ever felt so scared. I don't know why, but I just knew something was wrong."

She smiled back at him. "My not answering a phone call was probably the most normal thing that's happened to either of us in the past four days! But I'm glad you came when you did." She shivered, imagining how bad things could have gone if Marcos hadn't worried about her.

Imagine that. Someone worrying about her. It was almost as if they were a real couple, like she had someone in her life again to care what happened to her. The last time she could remember feeling protected and cared about this way was before her mom had died.

Or maybe that was unfair, because she had people in her life she mattered to. And she'd had other men who'd tried to get close, who'd fought for a real relationship with her. But even when she'd felt reciprocal attraction, none of them had offered her something she'd battle for. And now? After four days, she'd found someone worth any fight, because she couldn't imagine her life without Marcos.

As she stared at him with growing awareness, Marcos just kept stroking her cheek, his other hand low on her back. There was something both possessive and familiar about his touch, and Brenna laid her head on his shoulder before he saw panic spark in her eyes.

She'd promised him a trade-off: a look inside each other's houses. But what that really meant to her was much more complicated. She'd been offering him a relationship, a look inside her heart. And while only time would tell how things might work out between them, she was already involved.

What did she know about relationships? She'd avoided them most of her life. Not just the romantic type, but all connections that got too close. Was she even capable of letting someone in?

Growing up in foster care, bouncing from one place to another, always alone, she'd pushed back her fears that her mother's death had damaged her. She'd always figured that she had time to make changes, that eventually life would fall into place and those connections would, too.

But that hadn't happened, and fear rose up hard now that she would always be too broken to offer Marcos anything worth having.

"Hey." Marcos's soft voice penetrated her fears and he cupped her cheek, shifting her to face him. "What's wrong?"

How did she tell him her fears without scaring him off? Marcos had faced a lot of the same challenges she had, but he hadn't let them close him off. Instead, he'd formed a brotherly bond that was as strong as the blood bond she'd shared with her mom.

So, instead of answering, she pressed her lips to his and kissed him. She poured everything she was feeling into the kiss: her fear; her attraction to him; her admiration for who he'd become; even the love that shouldn't be possible after such a short time, but she could no longer deny. Once upon a time, it might have been a simple crush on a boy who'd shown her kindness when she needed it most in her life. But somehow, in the past few days, it had morphed into something much bigger, something she knew wasn't going to fade no matter what happened between them.

His fingers slid over her face, down the back of her neck, then glided up her arms. His lips caressed hers as though he was feeling the very same things, and hope exploded in Brenna's chest with such intensity that she had to pull back and gulp in a breath.

Then Marcos was scooting them both backward along the bed until they could lay on it, and Brenna suddenly didn't care how tired she was. She slid her fingers up underneath his sweater, loving the way his ab muscles tensed underneath her touch. She fused her lips back to his, and he growled in the back of his throat.

His hands locked on her hips as he pulled her tightly against him and kissed her with such an intensity that the room seemed to spin. Brenna grabbed fistfuls of his sweater and held on, letting the emotions crash over her, letting Marcos further into her heart.

When he finally lifted his head from hers, Brenna had lost all sense of time. He looked just as dazed, but then he gave her that big, dimpled grin that had sucked her in from the very first time she'd seen him.

"What do you say we get some sleep, then head out tomorrow and close this case, put this threat completely behind us? Then I want to come back here and finish this, when I have the strength to love you like you deserve."

Brenna's mouth went dry, and she nodded back at him until he tucked her against his chest. If this was Marcos without full strength, then she was going to need some sleep, too.

As she drifted off to sleep in his arms, she felt a smile tug her lips. Had his word choice been intentional? Because being loved by Marcos Costa was something she wanted desperately, and not just for one night.

For the rest of her life.

Chapter Twenty-One

Marcos woke slowly, becoming aware of bits of sunlight sneaking past the curtains, the unfamiliar bed, the woman curled up in his arms. His arms instinctively tightened, holding Brenna closer, and she stirred a little, only to snuggle closer still.

Every day should be like this. The thought shouldn't have caught him by surprise. He already knew he'd managed to fall in love with her. But it did surprise him. Love was one thing; forever was another. And yet...his heart was telling him Brenna should never have left his life in the first place.

He'd never thought he was a *forever* kind of guy. Marriage and family were fine for Andre and Cole—and he wanted that for both of his brothers. But he'd always figured that he'd spend his life spoiling nieces and nephews rotten, and chasing down bad guys in undercover roles across the world. He'd even applied to an open post in the Middle East a few months ago; now, he knew he'd be retracting it. Suddenly, nowhere seemed like it could possibly be more exciting than right beside Brenna.

Panic threatened and he shoved it down. He went unarmed into the remote hideouts of vicious drug lords. He could handle being in love with a commitment-phobic woman who ran headlong into danger herself.

"Mind over matter," he muttered to himself. He might not be able to change his natural wariness about relationships, but he could choose to jump into one anyway. Because if anyone was worth taking that chance for, it was Brenna Hartwell.

"What?" she mumbled sleepily.

"Nothing." He kissed the top of her head, then let himself hold her a minute longer before slipping out of bed.

Grabbing the cell phone he'd dropped on the dresser last night, Marcos opened the slider to the balcony, and a rush of cold air blasted into the room.

"Brrr," Brenna groaned, sitting up, but hauling the covers with her. "What are you doing?"

"Sorry. I was going to step outside and make a call." He grinned at the tangled mess of her hair, the sleepy half-mast of her eyes. "I didn't mean to wake you."

She made a face at him and finger-combed her hair. "Why are you smiling like that?" Not giving him a chance to answer, she added, "And close the door. I'm up."

He pushed it shut, then strode over to the bed, leaned across it and planted a kiss on her lips. "I'm smiling because you're ridiculously cute first thing in the morning." And she was.

As for him, he was practically giddy with happiness. His brothers were going to have a field day teasing him. He probably deserved it after the way he'd mercilessly teased them when they'd both fallen in love over the past few months.

She flushed and straightened her hair a little more, then said, "I'm pretty sure this is far from first thing in the morning, but thank you. Who are you calling?"

Marcos glanced at the time on his phone, realizing she was right. It was almost noon. But apparently no one had expected him in the office that morning, and even Jim was giving him a little breathing room. "I'm going to give Jim a call, see what the status is with Carlton."

She let the covers drop away and crawled across the bed toward him as he sat on the edge of the bed. "Speaker?"

"Sure." He let his gaze wander over her. She'd fallen asleep in jeans and a sweatshirt; he was still wearing what he'd had on in the mountains, and he realized he desperately needed a shower.

But she didn't seem to care as she looped her arms around his neck and rested her head against his back. "Maybe he's talking."

There wasn't a lot of hopefulness in her tone, and Marcos doubted Carlton had broken, either. But if he wasn't really in charge, would he be willing to risk going down for another man's empire? "Let's find out," he said, dialing Jim.

His partner picked up on the first ring. "Marcos? I wondered when you were gonna tear yourself away from your lady friend and call in."

Against his back, Marcos felt Brenna muffling her laughter. "You're on Speaker, man."

"Oh. Hi, Brenna. Sorry about that."

"No problem," she said, laughter in her voice.

Marcos got down to business. "So, what's the status?"

Jim sighed. "Well, the good news is that we caught Carlton's last bodyguard-slash-cook. The guy came after us with a butcher's knife, so he's in surgery right now, having a bullet taken out of his chest, but it looks like he'll pull through."

"And what about Carlton?"

"He's not talking. The guy knows he's going to be doing some major time. But I think he figures we've already got him on trying to kill a federal agent and a police officer, and maybe on killing his own guard—although we haven't found a body yet, which always makes a conviction challenging. So I'm sure he's decided, why hand over a drug charge, as well? Because we can try to get him on promises he made to you, but you know how that'll go."

"Yeah." In court, he'd claim that he was talking about some other kind of product, or that he was just joking. With no audio and video evidence like they would have had if the buy had actually gone through, it was unlikely to stick. "What about Jesse? Is he flipping on his uncle?"

"The kid is scared," Jim replied. "Scared of his uncle, scared of doing time, and honestly, at this point, he's scared of his own shadow. But I think you might get through to him. We know he thinks Carlton had his parents killed. That's pretty powerful motivation to turn on the guy."

Brenna's arms tightened around him at the mention of the car crash that had killed Jesse's family, and he didn't think she'd realized she'd done it. "Is there anything there?" Marcos asked. "Can we get that case reopened? Even if we can get Carlton life without parole on everything else, I'd still like him to pay for that, even if it's just another symbolic sentencing."

"We're going to talk to the local police about that. What do you think about coming in and talking to Jesse?"

"Later today," Marcos promised. "First, I need to pay my old foster parents a visit. Did Carlton give any sense that he *wasn't* running the show?"

There was a long pause. "No. You have reason to think he wasn't?"

"Maybe."

When Marcos didn't say more, Jim replied, "All right, well, do what you need to do with your foster parents and then give me a call. Keep me in the loop on this. You taking backup?"

"Yeah, Brenna's coming with me."

"Good. Hey, Brenna?"

She lifted her head from his back. "Yeah?"

"Take care of him for me, will you?"

Marcos twisted his head to look at her, and she smiled at him. "You got it."

THIS WAS HOME ONCE. Sort of.

Marcos stared at the empty lot where their foster home had once stood. Beside him, Brenna folded her uninjured hand in his.

Apparently, their foster parents had never rebuilt here after the fire. Eighteen years later, there was no evidence a house had ever stood there at all, except that it was one bare lot in a row of little houses. The grass was overrun with weeds, but it stood waist-high, browning leaves sprinkled across it in places.

It was hard to picture the worn-down two-story building where he'd come when he was seven years old. His most vivid memories of those days were of his brothers. Meeting them on that very first day when he'd faltered in the doorway, his only belongings clutched in a small backpack. Following them to the backyard when they'd gone to play a game of catch, thinking they hadn't seen him. His surprise and uncertainty when they'd called him over to join them. And then a bond he'd never had in his short years on this Earth.

And then there were the memories of Brenna. He'd known her only a few months, but the time was stamped into his brain. He didn't think he'd ever forget the sight of her on the stoop, tears watering over her eyes, her hair in braids and a nasty gash on her cheek from the car crash. He knew he'd never forget the way it had felt when he'd reached out and taken her hand—as though she was his reason for existing.

He turned to find her staring contemplatively

at the empty lot. "It's hard to believe this is where we met," she said softly.

He pressed a kiss to her lips. "Come on. Let's go see our old foster parents."

They'd known before coming here that their foster parents were long gone. But they hadn't moved far, and on the drive over, Marcos had felt his hands turning the wheel onto a familiar street. In the passenger seat, Brenna hadn't said a word, but he'd known she realized exactly where he was taking her.

Silently, they climbed back into his car, and he made the relatively short trip to their foster parents' new house. When he stopped in front of it, Marcos whistled and then double-checked the address he'd written down back at the hotel.

"Awfully nice place for someone who quit his factory job and supposedly just went to work in his son's business part-time," Brenna said, a hard edge to her voice as they climbed out of his car.

Marcos found it hard to believe that the man who'd taken him into his home for those five years was secretly a drug lord. But the house in front of them—easily five times the size of the little house where they'd crammed eight people back then—suggested he was into something more than he was officially reporting on his taxes. Especially since their foster mother had also quit her part-time work a few years later.

"Let's be ready for anything," Marcos said, and Brenna nodded, patting her hip. He knew that concealed under her sweatshirt was her service pistol. He was also carrying. Probably unnecessary with their foster parents, but if they were in league with Carlton in any way, they were more dangerous than they seemed.

They walked up the long entryway, and then Marcos knocked, hoping the Pikes would answer. The plan was to try to play it off as an innocent visit initially, in case their foster parents hadn't heard about Carlton. If necessary, he and Brenna would take a more official route, but right now, they had no evidence and nothing to get an arrest warrant.

The door swung open, and Marcos recognized their foster mother immediately. She'd aged gracefully, with streaks of silver through her light brown hair, and a regal stance to her that Marcos didn't remember from his childhood.

"Can I help you?" she asked.

"Uh, yes. I'm Marcos Costa. This is Brenna Hartwell. We were—"

"Oh my goodness," she cut him off. "From before the fire. Of course! Come in." She held the door wider, letting them pass.

Inside, Marcos glanced around curiously. The house was a far cry from the small place they'd packed in six foster kids. The floors were expensive, patterned hardwood in the entryway, a huge chandelier overhead. Disappointment filled him at the mounting suspicion that they were involved even more than he'd expected. Passing on foster kid information was bad enough; actually being the mastermind took the betrayal he was feeling to a whole new level. Although he didn't have any real bond with them, he still had fond feelings for the home, because of all that it had given him in his life: Andre, Cole and Brenna.

Their foster mother led them into a huge living room with a wall of windows looking out over a man-made lake, then gestured for them to take a seat on the big white sectional couch.

Brenna sat gingerly at the edge of the couch, and he sat beside her. "Is Mr. Pike here?" he asked.

"Yes, he is. Let me just get him." She fiddled nervously with her hair, then shook her head. "I can't believe you two. All grown up." She glanced between them, and added, "And dating now? Or married? It's a good thing you two didn't stay in that house like siblings."

Brenna nodded noncommittally, and their foster mother backed out of the room. The truth was, none of the kids in that house had felt like siblings to him, except Andre and Cole, no matter how long he'd lived there. Brenna hadn't been there very long, but his connection to her certainly hadn't been familial.

When their foster mother was out of the room, Brenna whispered, "What do you think?"

"She's definitely nervous," he replied, watching the doorway carefully. Although he didn't expect their foster father to suddenly appear with a weapon, he wasn't taking any chances.

But when Mr. Pike did appear a minute later, Marcos worked to keep his jaw from dropping. Their foster mother was leading him into the room, with a supportive hand on his back. Physically, he looked pretty good. A little hunched over from his years of hard labor, but the years didn't show on him otherwise.

Mentally was a different story. Even before his eyes locked on Marcos's, he could tell the man wasn't entirely there.

"Dementia," their foster mother explained, a little teary eyed. "Started about a year ago. He's got good days and bad. Today he probably won't understand who you are, but we'll try." Then she smiled at him and said, "Honey, you remember Marcos Costa—he lived with us about five years, back before the fire? And little Brenna Hartwell? She was there a few months."

"Marcos," he repeated. "And Brenna. Nice to meet you."

Their foster mother shook her head at them, then helped her husband settle into a chair. Then she took a seat and leaned forward, twisting her hands in her lap. "So tell me how you've been. It's so nice to see you after all these years."

Marcos shared a glance with Brenna. If their foster father had ever masterminded anything, that time was long gone. But the house they lived in was nicer than Marcos would have expected for someone who was just passing names for a payoff.

They were missing something. But what?

Chapter Twenty-Two

"Marcos and I just recently ran into each other again," Brenna told them, watching carefully for any reaction. Because *someone* had blown their cover at that mansion with Carlton, and she might have recognized Sara Lansky's voice on the phone, but she doubted the woman would have recognized *her.* And if she had, she would have only known her as a fellow social worker. And she wouldn't have known Marcos at all.

The leak had come from somewhere, and if it wasn't Mr. Pike... Brenna turned her gaze on Mrs. Pike, who was fiddling with the hem of her sweater. She'd been nervous since the moment they'd arrived, but Brenna found it hard to believe she would have collaborated with her husband's mistress. Unless maybe her husband had been in charge until the past year, and then his wife had reluctantly taken over in order to keep up their lifestyle.

Brenna frowned at the idea. It could fit, but she sensed that wasn't right, either.

"Oh, yes?" their foster mother said. "How did you reconnect?" She looked from Brenna to Marcos, seeming genuinely curious.

"Up in the mountains," Marcos said, sounding purposely vague.

"Oh. That's…unusual." Their foster mother returned to fiddling with her sweater. "And what about those other boys, the ones you were so close to?"

"Cole and Andre?" Marcos said. "They went into law enforcement, just like me."

"Law enforcement?" Her voice went up half an octave, then she coughed. "That's great. So, you're a police officer? I never would have imagined that."

"No," Brenna replied. "He's not a police officer. I am. Marcos works for the DEA."

"I see," she replied, and the nervousness seemed to fade, replaced by a wary distrust that blanked the expression on her face.

Next to her, Marcos leaned forward, glancing from Mrs. Pike to her husband, who didn't seem to be following the conversation at all. "So, you know why we're here."

"No," she said, her voice suddenly hard and cold. "I can't say that I do."

"Carlton Wayne White," Brenna supplied.

She shook her head. "I'm not familiar with him."

"How about Sara Lansky?" Brenna asked, and this time she got a reaction.

Mrs. Pike visibly twitched, her gaze darted to her husband, then back to them as she stood. "I think it's time for you to go."

"If we leave now, we'll be back with a warrant and a whole lot more agents," Marcos promised.

She folded her arms over her chest. "Then I guess that's what you'll have to do."

Marcos stood and Brenna did the same, but before Mrs. Pike shut the door behind them, Brenna told her, "Oh, in case you hadn't heard, we've got Carlton in custody."

The door didn't close fast enough to hide their foster mother's panicked expression.

Brenna stared at Marcos. "Well, she's involved."

"Yeah," Marcos agreed with a sigh. "I guess we'd better give Jim a call. I'm not sure how we're going to get that warrant, but we'd better figure something out before they run."

As they walked toward Marcos's car, Brenna glanced backward and saw their foster mother peeking through the shades, a phone pressed to her ear. When she spotted Brenna, she dropped the shades back into place.

"Something is off here, Marcos. I mean, she

obviously recognized Carlton's name, but when we first showed up, she seemed to genuinely want to know how we'd reconnected."

Marcos nodded grimly as they climbed back into his car. "I know. And if she was the one who'd blown our covers, then she'd already know exactly how that had happened."

"I THINK JESSE is going to work with us," Jim announced as soon as Marcos called him.

"That's good news," Brenna said, listening over the speaker, one eye still on the Pikes' house behind them. Marcos hadn't started his car, but had decided to sit out front for a while and see how the investigation at the DEA office was going, then plan their next move.

And it really was going to be *their* next move. She knew Marcos wasn't comfortable working with her yet—that he was resisting his natural urge to keep her as far away from danger as possible—but she also knew that if things were going to go anywhere between them, he'd have to get used to her job.

She was going to stay. She'd realized it while they were inside the Pikes' house, working to-gether. She didn't think she'd be going back undercover anytime soon, but *detective* was an idea that was gaining traction in her mind. Her mentor had been pushing her in that direction since the beginning, telling her that was where she belonged, and she was starting to think he was right.

As for the other place she belonged? She glanced at Marcos, looking serious as he listened to Jim explain that the kid hadn't made any promises, but had been asking about him. Jim felt confident he'd turn if Marcos could give him some guarantees. And she knew Marcos wanted to help the kid turn his life around.

She smiled and twined her hand with his, and he squeezed back as he told Jim, "We'll come into the office in a few minutes and talk to him then. We just got finished at our old foster parents' house."

"How'd that go?" Jim asked.

"Strange," Brenna supplied. "Our foster father has dementia. He wasn't following the conversation, but our foster mother definitely knew something. As for how much they were involved? We're not really sure."

"We're going to need to bring them both in," Marcos said.

"If he's sick—" Jim started.

"This man was up late at night, going over the names of foster kids he could sell out to a drug dealer in exchange for a cushy life. It may have been an accident, but he still started that fire."

In the pause that followed, Brenna could tell that Jim knew a lot about what had happened the night of the fire. How it had separated Marcos and his brothers, the scars it had left on his back.

But when he finally spoke, his words left her speechless. "It changed your life. You lost Brenna."

Marcos pressed his lips to her hand. "And now that I've found her again, I want to get some closure on the past. Whatever our foster father did, he still needs to pay for it."

"I understand," Jim said. "We're going to need more than a hunch, and Jesse never said anything about someone involved besides Carlton. But if we can flip Jesse…"

"It gives us leverage on Carlton," Marcos finished. "And he'll want to share the jail time if he can, rather than take the heat for everything himself."

"Exactly," Jim agreed.

"We're on our way," Marcos told him, disconnecting the call and pulling on his seat belt.

Brenna was doing the same when a Hummer squealed to a stop in front of them, blocking their exit. The driver got out, slammed the door and strode toward them, a furious expression on his face.

"He looks a lot like—" Brenna started.

"It's the Pikes' son," Marcos finished. "Trent."

"She must have called him when we left the house," Brenna said, watching Trent approach and doing the math. He'd be in his early forties now. He looked ageless, one of those guys who could be anywhere between thirty and fifty, with perfectly styled blond hair, chiseled cheekbones and an expensive wool coat. He'd managed to get the best of both parents' features, and apparently things had changed in eighteen years, because now he was showing up.

Trent stopped next to Marcos's window and knocked on it until Marcos rolled it down.

"What's wrong with you?" he yelled. "You come over here and harass my parents, accuse them of working with *drug dealers*? Are you crazy?"

"We're not harassing anyone," Marcos replied calmly. "We just needed explanations for some inconsistencies about your father's access to the foster care system."

"Foster care! Right. So, this is the thanks you give them for taking you into their home, raising you like you were actually their kids instead of street trash no one wanted?"

"Street trash?" Marcos repeated, sounding both offended and incredulous. "Is that what you think of foster kids? Is that why you think it's fine to use them however you want?"

Trent jerked backward, but recovered quickly.

"I don't know what you're talking about, and I want you out of here, now."

"Let me ask you something, Trent. Does the name Sara Lanksy mean anything to you?"

"Yeah, my father's mistress. So my dad's not perfect. Guess what? No one is." He stabbed a finger toward Marcos's face. "You leave them alone. I just left my wife by herself at brunch to deal with this nonsense. If I have to do it again, you're going to regret it. And your little badge there isn't going to save you this time."

He stomped back to his vehicle and peeled away, leaving Brenna to stare at Marcos in disbelief. "Did he really just say *this time*?"

"Yeah, he did. And if Carlton sent pictures of us from the mansion to anyone in this family, they'd all be able to recognize us."

Brenna frowned. "And get access to what we really do?"

"Someone who's been secretly running a drug operation of this size for twenty years has connections."

Brenna considered that, mulling over the idea of Trent being involved—and whether he'd gotten pulled in because of his father, or vice versa. "He didn't even go inside to check if they were okay."

"Yeah," Marcos agreed, his gaze following the Hummer as it spun around a corner. "And yet, eighteen years ago, I'm not even sure he would have done this much. You think he's protecting them or protecting the business?"

"It sure seems like both," Brenna said. It had never occurred to her to consider Trent, but it made a lot of sense. He could get the information from his dad and pass it on to Carlton, then Carlton could use it to build his empire.

"I agree," Marcos said. "But is he doing Carlton's bidding or is Carlton a figurehead?"

"Hang on," Brenna replied, texting Victor at the station. Less than a minute later he came back with a reply.

"Victor says Trent's lifestyle doesn't come even close to matching his tax returns."

"That was fast," Marcos said.

She grinned. "Yeah, you'll like Victor. He's got a way with computers. And he's the one who convinced me to become a cop."

Marcos leaned toward her, dropping a kiss on her lips that made her anxious to wrap this case up and take him up on his promise from last night. A shiver of anticipation ran through her at the thought, and he grinned, his dimples on full display, like he could read her mind.

"Maybe they're partners," Marcos said. "Carlton is perfect for the front man. He's got the sort of personality that likes being feared. And remember eighteen years ago, the way

Mrs. Pike talked about her son? All the bad influences he hung around?"

Brenna nodded. "And how he was a genius."

"Yeah, well, that might have been a bit of an exaggeration, but whoever ran this organization for the past twenty years is really savvy."

Brenna nodded back at him. "Probably savvier than Carlton Wayne White."

"I think we just found our mastermind."

"Then let's go and get him."

"Maybe you should think about making the leap over to DEA," Marcos suggested as he pulled away from the curb. "We could work together like this all the time."

"Yeah, I'm not sure undercover work is for me," Brenna replied.

"Carlton thought you were a natural," Marcos teased, shooting her a smile as he left the Pikes' neighborhood and turned onto the freeway.

"We just decided Carlton wasn't all that smart," Brenna joked. "Besides…" She squeezed his hand, still tucked in his as he drove one-handed. "Doesn't the DEA have rules about co-workers dating?"

"Not to mention spouses," Marcos added, and he said it so easily, so casually, as if it was a foregone conclusion.

Brenna's head spun at the idea, and panic tightened her chest. Marriage. Was she cut out for that?

Then she glanced over at Marcos's strong profile, and the panic started to subside. If anyone could make her want to promise her life to him, it was Marcos.

In fact, the more she thought about it, the more right it seemed. A smile started to bloom, and the panic in her chest exploded into unfettered joy. Marriage to Marcos. It might be a little scary, but there was suddenly no doubt. That's what she wanted for her future.

She probably should wait until they finished the investigation, until they were back in that hotel, making good on Marcos's promise, to tell him. Not driving on the freeway, knowing in their hearts who all the major players in this drug organization were, but still needing to prove it. But the words wanted to escape, and she couldn't hold them in one minute longer.

"Marcos, I lo—" she started, then her gaze darted up to the rearview mirror and she screamed as a huge dark vehicle raced toward them. "Watch out!" she screamed, but it was too late.

The Hummer slammed into the back of Marcos's car, and everything seemed to move in slow motion as the back end of the car lifted off the ground. Then they were spinning, out of control, heading for the concrete divider in the center of the freeway.

Chapter Twenty-Three

The air bag deployed, smacking her in the face hard enough to disorient her as Brenna clutched the armrests in a death grip and the car spun wildly.

Next to her, Marcos was grappling for control, trying to maneuver around his own airbag and pull the car out of the spin before it slammed into the divider.

It started to slow, and then she saw the Hummer, coming at them again. This time, when she looked behind her, she could actually see Trent behind the wheel, his face twisted in a nasty grimace as he barreled toward them.

The car lurched forward as Marcos gave it a little gas, trying to stop the spin and get out of the way at the same time, but Brenna knew it was too late. She braced for the next hit, but it didn't matter.

The Hummer smacked into them again,

squishing her against the air bag before her seat belt yanked her back, making it hard to breathe. Beside her, Marcos made a sound of pain, and then the Hummer hit again.

This time, the car flipped. Her stomach dropped as up became down, and then they slammed back into the ground. She felt the jolt through her entire body, but only once in her life had she felt this helpless as the car slid forward on its roof.

Marcos dangled upside down next to her, his eyes closed, and when she heard a wailing sound, it took a minute to realize it was her. Instantly, she was transported back eighteen years to another car crash, to looking into the front seat and seeing her mom, already gone. She couldn't survive watching another person she loved die.

As the car finally came to a stop, Brenna struggled against her seat belt, but thought better of it just before she unsnapped it and fell on her head. Instead, she stretched left, trying to touch Marcos.

"Marcos? Marcos? Are you okay?"

Her voice sounded distant, and she blinked as he went blurry. Swiping her hand over her eyes to wipe away tears, she was surprised when it came back bloody. Her head pounded, and she realized she had a nasty gash in her hairline, but it didn't matter. All that mattered right now was Marcos opening his eyes.

"Marcos!" She grabbed his arm, shaking it, hoping for a response. When there was none, she fumbled to press her fingers to his wrist, searching for a pulse. But she couldn't tell over the thundering of her own heart, the pain exploding all over her body.

"Marcos!" she shouted, and this time he groaned in response.

Relief made it hard to breathe, and her hand shook as she took his. "Are you okay?"

His eyes opened and he stared back at her. Pain was reflected in those blue-gray depths, but he was alive.

This wasn't like eighteen years ago. Tears filled her eyes instantly, the rush of them so heavy it was hard to see.

"It's okay," Marcos rasped. "We're okay."

Behind him, through the cracked side window, Brenna spotted cars swerving to a stop. But much closer, a pair of expensive loafers moved leisurely toward the vehicle and Brenna swore. "He's coming."

She braced her hand on the roof, now underneath her, to help break her fall, then pressed down on the seat-belt release. Nothing happened.

Tugging harder, Brenna tried again as Marcos did the same. Beside her, he slammed into the ceiling with a sickening thud, partially bracing his fall, and let out a groan. He was twisting to reach for the weapon he had holstered at his hip, but she could tell something was going wrong even before he lifted his sweatshirt and she could see that the gun had come free during the crash.

Then, Trent's face was filling the side window, a satisfied grin on his face. He mouthed a mocking *Sorry* as he pulled something from his pocket.

Expecting a gun, Brenna gave up on the seat belt and reached for her own weapon, but it was wedged between her and the seat belt, jammed tight.

Then, Trent's hand came back and Brenna's pulse took off. Instead of a gun, he held a match.

Yanking at the seat belt was useless, so Brenna shoved herself closer toward Marcos, her eyes watering at the intense pain that ripped through her side. Ignoring it, she yanked her gun free and swung it toward Trent, still grinning in the window.

Angling her arms in front of her awkwardly, she fired just as Trent struck the match and tossed it.

Then the front of the car went up in flames.

THE WORLD IN front of him was on fire.

Marcos reacted instinctively as smoke billowed toward him and flames sucked at the windshield. He jerked his feet away from the front of the car and grabbed the door handle, trying to shove it open.

It stuck, refusing to budge, and Marcos gasped in a desperate lungful of air, even though he knew he needed to try not to breathe the smoke. Through the window, he could see Trent on the ground, eyes wide but staring sightlessly at the sky.

But they were still in trouble. The people who'd stopped on the freeway had kept their distance—either because of the gunshot or the fire. The smoke was starting to turn gray, and he could feel the heat seeping in from the hood.

He tried to keep the panic at bay, tried not to remember the feeling when he'd lifted his head in that house all those years ago after falling on the stairs. But it came back to him, the sight of the flames blocking his exit, his brothers both gone.

At least in that terrifying moment, he'd known they'd made it out of the fire, even if he didn't. He turned to look at Brenna, and his fear seemed to quadruple. "Brenna, does your door open?"

She grabbed the handle, twisting awkwardly,

still hanging upside down, tethered by her seat belt, trying to kick it when it only moved centimeters.

"I...can't...get...it," she wheezed.

Marcos swore and climbed into the back seat awkwardly, his head throbbing and his vision unsteady. "Come on. Move away from the fire. The back isn't as crumpled. Maybe these doors will...yes!" He shoved the door and it popped open.

"Brenna!" He glanced back, and she twisted her head to look at him, tears in her eyes.

"I'm stuck."

He pushed his head and chest through the small space between the two front seats, reaching around her and grabbing hold of her seat belt. Pressing hard on the release button, he yanked as hard as he could. Nothing.

Bracing his feet on the roof beneath him, Marcos tried again, and this time, Brenna wrapped her hands over his and tugged, too. He sucked in another breath, choking on smoke instead as he yanked again and again. But no matter how hard they pulled, the seat belt didn't come loose.

"Go," Brenna said, her gaze swiveling from the hood of the car, now engulfed in flames, a thick black smoke rising from it, back to him.

"No way," Marcos said, fighting the panic

making it hard to breathe. Or maybe that was just the smoke. It no longer seemed to matter that the back door was open, letting in air, because smoke was filling the interior fast.

Way off in the distance, Marcos heard sirens approaching, but he knew they weren't going to make it in time.

"The car's going to blow," Brenna told him, her voice strangely calm, even though there was fear and sadness in her eyes. "You need to get out."

"I don't suppose you have another butter knife on you," he said, ignoring her ridiculous suggestion.

"Marcos, go!" Brenna shouted, then choked on the smoke. She coughed violently, then insisted, "I want you to go. You're not dying in here."

"Neither are you," he promised, searching the car for something—anything—to saw through the seat belt and get her free. But there was nothing.

He kept searching, reaching past her to yank open the glove box, and swearing at the burning heat that seared through his hand. But the only things in his glove box were a compass, a map of the Appalachian Mountains and a spare cell phone.

"Marcos." She grabbed his hand in hers,

holding on tight and effectively stopping his desperate search. "I love you. I've loved you since I was eleven years old."

He started to respond, but she kept going. "And I'll never forgive you if you don't get out of this car right now."

"Brenna," he whispered, tears clouding his vision because he knew she was right about one thing. The car was going to blow any second, and he couldn't get her out.

But he wasn't leaving without her, either. "We're a team," he told her, then scooted closer.

She lifted her other hand to shove him away from her, trying to force him to leave, and he spotted it: the gun still clutched in her hand.

Yanking it away from her, he tugged her toward him, then reached around her and aimed the gun at the seat-belt mechanism.

"No!" she yelled. "The fuel. It could spark!"

Marcos fired anyway, and then Brenna fell toward him and he grabbed hold of her and tugged her into the back seat. He could tell he was hurting her—something was wrong with her side—but he kept going, feeling blindly for the open back door as the thick smoke got even blacker.

And then, somehow, they were falling onto the cold, hard pavement. But Marcos knew that wasn't good enough.

The car was going to go.

He shoved himself to his feet and ran, half carrying Brenna as she stumbled along beside him. Then he pushed them both to the ground and covered her body with his as an explosion *boomed* behind them, and pieces of metal and fire rained from the sky.

Beneath him, Brenna groaned and rolled so she was facing him, the pinched expression on her face telling him she'd broken at least one rib. Then her arms were around his neck as she choked out, "We're a good team."

"I love you, too," he said in return, then wiped soot away from her mouth and kissed her.

Epilogue

The boy in the doorway smiled at her. It was tentative, but understanding, and it made dimples pop on both cheeks. Then he held out his hand and Brenna took it, and somehow, she knew nothing would ever be the same again.

"Marcos."

"I'm here."

Brenna frowned, trying to make sense of what was happening as her past mingled with her present, and she opened her eyes. She was lying in a hospital bed, and Marcos was sitting in a chair beside her, his hand tucked in hers.

"What happened?"

He leaned closer, looking concerned, and she saw the hastily cleaned soot still clinging to the edges of his face and his clothes. "Trent hit our car and—"

"I know that," Brenna rasped. "Why am I in the hospital?" The last thing she remembered was being flattened to the pavement by Marcos, then him whispering something to her before he kissed her.

"You love me." She remembered his words.

He grinned, and there were those dimples. The man was so much more than she ever could have imagined in the eighteen years they'd been separated, and yet, he was exactly how she'd expected him to grow up on that very first day. Strong and kind and exactly who she needed.

"I do," he whispered, then he got serious and told her, "You passed out on the freeway after we hit the ground. They admitted you to check you out, but everything looks okay. You have a few cracked ribs and a lot of bruises. They stitched up a bad cut on your head, and they gave you oxygen because of the smoke inhalation, but you'll be out of here by tomorrow."

"And you?"

"I'm fine. Some burns on one hand, but I've been through this before. They're just covered in ointment and wrapped. Same deal with the smoke inhalation, but nothing that won't heal."

"When we were in that car, I was flashing back to the time with my mom…"

"I know," Marcos said softly. "I'm sorry."

"And then the fire…" It had to be his worst nightmare come back to life, too, and yet, he'd stayed with her.

"We got out," Marcos said simply. "And when Jim told Jesse what had happened to us, the kid spilled everything. He didn't want any part of that, said he knew we'd tried to help him get away."

"So, was Trent in charge or Carlton?"

Marcos shrugged. "Jesse wasn't sure, but he thought they had a dysfunctional partnership that was getting more and more uneven. It sounds like once upon a time, Trent had all the power, but Carlton was trying to make a play for it. And Carlton still isn't talking. Jim agrees with us that they were in it together from the very beginning. Carlton's power came from being the face of the organization, and Trent's came from his foster care connection. It's why Carlton was recruiting you. He knew Trent's connection through his father was retiring, so he wanted to grab some of that power for himself."

"What about the Pikes?"

"They're talking, too, since their son's death. They're claiming they didn't know what he was really doing with the names, but we're not buying it. I'm not sure what's going to happen because of Mr. Pike's medical needs, but they're going to face time."

"Good." She squeezed his hand, and he scooted his chair even closer to the bed. "They should pay for what they did to all those kids. And for what happened to us all those years ago."

"I'm glad we found our way back to each other," Marcos told her. "Because—"

A knock at the door cut him off, and then Cole and Andre peeked in. "How's she doing?"

"Awake," Marcos told them. "Come in."

"Thank goodness," Cole said, and Andre added, "We've got company."

Brenna shifted a little, pressing the button on the remote beside her to lift her bed so she was half sitting. She grimaced at the pain in her ribs, but it was worth it to see everyone right now. "Who?"

"The rest of the family," Cole said. "This is my fiancée, Shaye." He indicated a tall redhead with a friendly smile.

"And this is my fiancée, Juliette," Andre added, gesturing to the brunette holding his hand.

"Nice to meet you both," Brenna said. Normally, she'd be self-conscious about the fact that she was laid out from injuries and still feeling emotionally wrecked from being trapped in that car with Marcos. But somehow, this group made her feel instantly at ease. As if they were her family, too.

"We're glad you're awake," Andre said. "And that the case is finally over."

"Well, we've got all the major players in custody," Marcos corrected him. "But the investigation isn't over. I want the rest of his organization, too."

"And the kids he had running drugs for him," Brenna added. "I don't want them falling through the cracks again. I want to find a way to help them into normal lives, if we can."

Marcos smiled softly at her. "I've been thinking about that transition program you were pretending to set up for Carlton."

"What about it?"

"What if it was real?"

Brenna nodded back at him, knowing that she was going to find a way to do it. She had a lot of free time outside of the job. It wouldn't be easy, but she had a feeling the things most worth doing weren't easy.

"I think between the two of us, we can garner a lot of support for a program like that," Marcos said.

"Between the six of us," Cole spoke up. "That's how family works. We're a team."

Tears welled up so fast that Brenna couldn't stop them from spilling over. *Family.* It had been eighteen long years since she'd had anyone to call family.

"Hey," Marcos said, wiping the tears away. "Don't start crying yet. I haven't even gotten to tell you what I wanted to say before my brothers came in."

A surprised laugh snuck out. "You're going to make me cry?"

"Happy tears, I hope," Marcos said, suddenly looking nervous. And then he was reaching into his pocket and telling her, "So, I remember you telling Carlton that you liked diamonds..."

He flipped open a box and a ring was staring back at her.

Brenna's mouth dropped open, and she looked up into his eyes, surprised and scared and happier than she thought she'd ever felt in her life. "It's only been a few days," she whispered. "Are you sure?"

"I love you," he answered, as if it was the simplest thing in the world. "And after all these years, after thinking I might lose you in that car, there's one thing I know for sure. It's something I think I knew the minute I saw you in the doorway of that foster house. Home is always going to be wherever you are."

"I love you, too," she said, and she realized it didn't matter that it had been less than a week since she'd first seen him all grown up. She'd never stopped loving that boy with the dimples, and she was never going to stop loving the man he'd become.

She had a lifetime to learn all the little details about him. And she knew it was going to be the best journey she'd ever take.

She held out a shaky hand for the ring and Marcos grinned at her, his dimples popping. "So is that a *yes*?"

"Yes."

Then, the ring was on her finger and Marcos was kissing her and there was a loud *pop* behind him.

When she pulled back, she saw Andre holding up an open bottle of champagne and Cole pulling out glasses.

"To family," Marcos said, his gaze never leaving hers.

"To family," she agreed, and pulled him down for another kiss.

* * * * *

Get 2 Free Books,
Plus 2 Free Gifts—
just for trying the Reader Service!

HP17R2